State of Vengeance

Collapse Series #6

Summer Lane

To everyone who gave me a chance to prove them wrong.

Thanks for the motivation.

Prologue

"Come on, Harry," Sophia said, smiling slightly. "Be serious."

She sat with her back pressed against the wall, staring at the darkened room of sleeping prisoners. Moonbeams fell through the high windows, across the old eighth-grade laboratory counters. People were asleep on the floors, twisted and curled into odd angles, all weak attempts to ward off the biting cold.

"I am *being serious.*"

Harry's teeth were a flash of white against the darkness. Even after being an enslaved laborer for several weeks, he still managed to look dashing. His dark, curly hair was beginning to grow out again, despite the initial haircut every prisoner had received upon arriving at the gates.

"Cassidy was right," Sophia said and sighed. "We have to wait and look for an opportunity to escape...we can't make *an escape.* Omega will kill us otherwise...Kameneva sure as hell will, too."

"Kamaneva, Omega." Harry waved his hand. "It doesn't matter. They're just pawns in a much bigger game. If we can offer them something important...something that they cannot resist..." He tilted his head. "She spoke with me."

"Who? Cassidy?"

"No. Kamaneva." Harry leaned closer to Sophia. Her mocha skin was covered with goosebumps. She rubbed her arms in attempt to warm them. "She offered us a way out."

Sophia raised her eyebrows.

"Like I said before," she replied. "Be serious."

"I'm not lying. She's offering rewards to prisoners who have news of mutinies, escapes...everything." Harry shrugged. "If you report rumors, gossip—anything—you can get on her good side. Avoid death a little longer."

Sophia opened her mouth to speak, then shut it.

"It seems...wrong," she whispered at last.

"It's survival."

"But everyone here is enslaved, Harry! If somebody is planning to escape – how could you possibly turn them in? Give them a chance to be free."

Harry rolled his eyes.

"Ah, you miss the point."

"What point?"

"Survival of the fittest." Harry leveled his gaze, staring at something across the room. "Only the most deadly predator can survive in a world like this."

Sophia swallowed a lump in her throat.

"Omega is a predator," she said quietly.

"Yes," Harry answered. "Become a predator, or become the prey."

Sophia shuddered.

Harry pulled a loose piece of thread from his shirt. He held it between his fingers, suddenly pulling it apart. The broken pieces drifted to the floor.

"No one will survive unchanged," he whispered. "We are doomed, all of us."

Chapter One

Monterey Bay, California – Pacific Northwest Alliance Stronghold

The ocean is like me. Calm and collected on the outside, but beneath the surface, churning and full of uncontained fury. I curl my fingers around the railing, standing on the back porch of a medical clinic on the edge of the city. The coastline is mired with thick, black smoke. Sirens scream in the distance. Two fighter jets twist over my head, ripping through the sound barrier, making my ears ring.

I take a deep breath. I stare at my hands.

Blood is crusted beneath my fingernails. Bruises line my jaw. I feel dry, numb. I lick my lips as the cold ocean breeze touches my cheeks. I feel like I should be crying, but I am too tired. I feel like I should be horrified, but I am too accustomed to war.

I glance over my shoulder. The medical clinic is a small, squat building, two stories high, on the edge of the town. I can clearly see the Monterey Peninsula. United States Navy vessels are bobbing in the harbor. Coast Guard cutters patrol the shoreline. The rumble and roar of military vehicles traveling up and down the roads is a steady, rhythmic sound that I am used to.

But it does not calm the storm within me.

"Cassidy."

I turn sharply, meeting Chris's stern, electric green eyes. He is worn down. His black clothes are torn in places. His hair is hanging in strands to his shoulders. His AR-15 is strapped across his back. Ruggedly handsome, but tired.

"Where's Harry?" I ask curtly.

"In the interrogation chamber." He walks to the railing, placing his fists on the wood. "What do you see out there, Cassie?"

"A whole lot of water," I reply.

"And what else?"

I pause before answering.

"Omega," I say at last. "They're coming back."

*

The world is a battleground. One year ago, an electromagnetic pulse destroyed the technological infrastructure of the United States, taking down all traces of modern civilization. This attack – staged by a mysterious shadow enemy called Omega – tore apart the fabric of society. Omega invaded. A million-man foot army pushed into the West Coast. The United States military struggled. Millions of people died.

I once lived in Los Angeles. I once was an average, everyday girl.

Now I am a Commander and a senator in the post-apocalyptic warzone of California, fighting for the preservation of life and hope in this state. Omega, the shadow army arisen from the chaos, is my enemy. My allies lay in the militias, in groups like the Freedom Fighters and the Mountain Rangers. My love lies with Commander Chris Young and my friends: Uriah, Andrew and so many others.

But I have been betrayed.

Betrayed by my best friend, Sophia Rodriguez, and now she is dead.

The cost of war is high. Standing firm for what you believe in is hard.

In my case, standing up for my beliefs has caused me nothing but suffering.

I am not alone. Chris – the most respected leader in the militias – is ever loyal and capable. I love him more than anything, and it is his love that has kept me alive this long. My father, a militia commander as well, went MIA when Omega bombed the Sacramento Capitol Building a few weeks ago. I must assume that he is dead. I have seen friends die. I have seen children die.

I have seen Omega's ruthless brutality and cold menace firsthand.

I have suffered, but I am a fighter.

I have lost, but I will win in the end.

This is just the beginning of the next chapter.

*

My hands are shaking. I am furious.

I storm down the hallway, bypassing guards and officers and wounded soldiers. It smells like blood here;

the screams of soldiers who have been burned or mutilated in battle echo off the walls, searing my ears.

I shove the metal doors at the end of the hall open. They hit the wall with a bang and I surge forward. Uriah True and Devin May are standing near a one-way window in a dark room. They whip around when I walk in.

"Cassidy?" Uriah asks. He reads me instantly. "What's wrong?"

I look through the window. Harry is sitting in a metal chair in the center of the empty interrogation chamber. He is staring at the wall.

"Have you talked to him yet?" I ask, my voice tight.

"No, we're going to, but..." Uriah trails off. "Cassidy, don't—"

I shove past him and round the corner. I open the door to the interrogation chamber. It opens out. I step inside, shut it behind me, and I set my deathly glare on Harry.

"Ah, Cassidy," he says. "How refreshing to see your smiling face."

I cross the room, grab his collar, and slam my knee under his chin, sending him careening off the chair, onto the floor. He hits the ground hard. Blood dribbles down the sides of his mouth. I grab the metal chair, spin it backward and shove it under the handle of the door, effectively locking us in.

I can hear Uriah banging on the door from the other side.

I ignore him.

All I see is red.

I kick Harry again. He rolls onto his back, bringing his arms up to block me. I force his hands away and grab the fabric of his shirt.

"Cassidy, stop!" Uriah yells.

I can hear him and Devin forcing the door open. Harry just looks at me, his baleful, beautiful blue eyes boring straight into mine. Angry, hurt tears slide down my face. I pull him upright and crouch close to his face.

"She's dead because of *you*," I say.

Harry doesn't answer.

"I hate you," I tell him. "I will always hate you."

To my shock, his face displays a profound look of sadness. He suddenly stops struggling against me and he says, "I'm sorry it had to be this way, Cassie."

I shove him forward and slam his head against the ground.

He is out cold.

"Don't call me Cassie," I mutter.

The door to the interrogation room bursts open and Devin and Uriah rush in. They look at Harry, then at me.

"Is he dead?" Uriah asks, breathing hard.

I shake my head.

Devin kneels down and checks Harry's pulse.

"He's fine." He looks at me. "What the *hell* is wrong with you? You almost killed a valuable prisoner of war."

I press my lips firmly together.

"This is about Sophia," Uriah says, never taking his gaze off me. "I know it hurts, Cassidy."

I wipe the hot, salty tears from my cheeks, embarrassed.

"Cassidy, don't go—"

I turn on my heel and walk out the door.

I am not ashamed that I have shed tears.

I am not ashamed that I almost killed Harry.

I am ashamed because I didn't.

*

I sit on a chair in the middle of an empty, dark room. I stare at the one-way window of the interrogation chamber. Harry is not there – he is in a cell somewhere. I keep my arms crossed, my expression taut. There is so much anger inside me.

I have been angry before, but this is different.

This is raging, physical. I can feel the fury pulsing through my veins and pounding in my ears. It is consuming, and I know that if I am not careful, it will eat me alive.

At this point, I'd almost welcome it.

The door to the room opens. A narrow slit of light slips across the darkness and then disappears as it closes again. I don't even have to look up to know that it is Chris. No one walks as softly as him, and no one exudes such a powerful presence.

"Cassidy, what are you doing?" he asks, his voice soft.

I shrug.

"I know you hate him," he continues. "But he's just one man."

I don't remove my gaze from the glass.

"Cassidy." Chris touches my shoulder. I look up. His handsome face is bathed in shadows. "What happened to Sophia wasn't your fault. It was her own choice."

I slide my hands down to my knees.

"I know," I say. "I just...feel empty."

"No." Chris gets down on one knee, eye level with me. "You feel angry. Because someone you loved is dead. I know that feeling, Cassidy. It can destroy you. Don't let it hurt you – use it against itself. Use it against Omega."

I rest my hand on his cheek, smiling sadly.

"People keep dying," I whisper. "My dad's MIA, and now Sophia is dead." I shake my head. "It's going to get worse and worse."

"This is war," Chris replies. "And you're right: it only gets worse." He takes my hand, kisses it, and holds it against his chest. "But then it gets better, in the end."

"If we're still alive," I sigh.

"We will be."

"There's no guarantee."

"Life is unpredictable, but I have no intention of dying, and let's face it: you're too stubborn to get killed." He grins. "And I love you for it."

Despite myself, I laugh a little.

"So. Are you going to start charging by the hour or should I just tip you?" I ask.

"I survive on tips," he replies, kissing me. It's a warm kiss. A kiss of kindness and comfort. "You can tip me as much as you want."

I stand up, slowly.

"I just keep thinking about the way that she looked when I left her up there on the roof," I say. "She looked so broken. I didn't know that girl."

"She *was* broken," Chris answers, draping his strong arm around my shoulders. "But *you're* stronger than that. Omega is afraid of you – of *us*. Sophia thought she'd found an escape. The truth is, there isn't one. We're all stuck in this situation. You just have to pick the right side. That's all that matters."

I tilt my head up, kissing the bottom of Chris's chin.

"You're too optimistic sometimes," I mutter.

"I try," he shrugs.

"Don't let it go to your head."

"Too late." He cups my cheek and brushes his lips across mine. "It already has."

I ask, "What are we going to do with Harry?"

Chris thinks about this.

"After we've squeezed every bit of information out of him," he replies, "we'll try him according to the law and execute him, just like we would anyone else."

I nod.

"His death won't bring Sophia back to life," Chris warns. "Remember that. Don't get hooked on revenge, Cassidy. It's not healthy."

I say nothing.

The door to the chamber opens, spilling light everywhere. Uriah squints in the darkness. "Ah, sorry to interrupt," he says, looking slightly embarrassed. "But the militia leaders are meeting. There are reports that Omega is regrouping."

My heart sinks.

"Great," I say. "We don't even get twenty-four hours of peace."

"Well, this *is* a warzone," Uriah answers.

Chris takes my hand and we enter the hallway together.

I am struck by the feeling that something is about to happen. What that something is, I have no idea. But the feeling is there. I have had premonitions before. I'm not superstitious, but my instincts have never been wrong.

I look at Chris.

"What?" he asks, raising an eyebrow.

"Something's coming," I say. "I can feel it."

Uriah opens the front door. We step into the coolness of evening.

"I know," he answers. "I can feel it, too."

Chapter Two

"They'll be back," I say.

My voice is firm. I do not hesitate.

I am standing in a room full of militia commanders and lieutenants. Among them are Chris Young, Uriah True, Vera Wright, Anita Vega and Devin May. In the back of the room, in the corner, a small girl with midnight-black hair is standing beside a beautiful German Shepherd. It is Elle Costas and her bomb dog, Bravo.

"Of course they'll be back," Vera replies. The hollows of her cheekbones are dark. Her eyes are bloodshot, and her blond hair is matted. "They've got *thousands* – if not *millions* – of more troops to send. This is a temporary victory."

"We don't have enough troops," Devin says. His white-blond hair is shaved down to the scalp. He is tall and imposing. A true Navy SEAL, just like Chris. "We have a few thousand right now, but that's it. Even the Pacific Northwest Alliance can't keep Omega out forever."

"So we need *more* troops?" Anita interjects. "We're already massing all of our soldiers. Do you know how many people we *lost* last night? How many soldiers *I lost?*"

I swallow a lump in my throat. I fold my arms across my chest to hide my trembling hands. It has been too long since I have eaten or rested, and my exhaustion is beginning to show.

"Too many," Chris replies, his voice calm and steady. When he speaks, people stop and listen. They always have, they always will. "We lost many good men and women last night. Securing Monterey came at a high price, one that the militias paid in blood."

"Once again, the militias have saved the day," Vera snorts. "Our *partnership* with the Pacific Northwest Alliance didn't do a *damn* thing."

"It did *something*," I reply. "It brought in the Navy and the Air Force."

"They were too late!"

"But they came."

"There's not enough of them to keep Omega from coming back. They're regrouping. We're screwed."

I look at Chris. He looks at me.

I say, "We're doing the best we can with what we have."

"That sounds like something a teacher would tell a classroom," Anita retorts, flipping her long, glossy black hair over her shoulder. She is the Commander of the Mexican militia group Coyotes, and while she is an incredibly adept fighter, she has a hot temper...a lot like me.

"Cool down, Anita," Chris tells her, raising an eyebrow.

Anita snorts.

"We've fortified the defenses around the city," he continues. "The Navy is here. The Air Force is patrolling

16

the coastline. We're safe for now. I suggest that we rest and meet here in the morning."

Silence.

"Fine," Vera says, clipped. "I'm starved, anyway."

She turns on her heel and flounces out of the room. I feel bad for her – she is worried about Andrew, one of our best friends. He was shot last night by Sophia right before she died...he is currently in the medical building, recovering from his wounds.

"Excuse me?"

The voice is so quiet, we hardly notice it. I turn and see Elle standing very close to me. She is as quiet as a ghost, and I hadn't even seen her creep up on me. Her crystal-blue eyes survey the room. Anita and the rest of the leaders gathered here wait for her to speak.

"Omega is like a predator," she says. "They wait until we can't see them, and then they attack. Because if we know they're coming, they know that we'll just pull back or hide or defend ourselves, right?"

Anita rolls her eyes.

"I did not come here to listen to a *child* talk about warfare," she says.

I give Anita a scathing glare, and she falls silent once more.

"Go on, Elle," Chris encourages.

"I guess what I'm trying to say is," Elle continues, taking a deep breath, "well, while we're all so busy waiting for them to come back to the coastline in ships...what if they're coming up behind us? What if this is just another distraction?"

Uriah shakes his head.

"That's a good point, Elle," he answers, "and we've considered that. But we only have so many defenses. We've got to concentrate them where we know Omega will hit the hardest."

Elle wrinkles her brow, but says nothing. I wonder what she's thinking, this mysterious young girl from the city. As the leaders disperse and leave the room, spent and exhausted from the Battle of Monterey, Chris and I linger. I exchange a glance with him and catch Elle as she is headed out the door.

"Elle?" I say.

She looks at me.

"What's bothering you?" I ask. "What are you thinking?"

For a long moment, I think that she is going to bolt. She looks a little like a deer caught in headlights. Her grip on Bravo's harness tightens, and then she relaxes, like she remembers that she is talking to me – someone she can trust.

"I just have this feeling," she says. "I feel like this is cat and mouse. They're playing with us. They want us dead, we're in their way. Something bigger is coming. I can feel it. Fighting with us all the time seems like a waste of their resources. I don't know..." She looks at me. "Can't you *feel* it?"

I stare at her. A cold, icy chill slips into the pit of my stomach.

I have felt it. So has Chris.

"Yeah," I say quietly. "I can."

*

We do not go back to the Naval Postgraduate School. The grounds are littered with rubble, and I do not want to look at the place where Sophia died. We retreat to old military housing units near the seashore. It is heavily guarded here. Chris and I arrive in a Jeep. We drive in silence. I am too exhausted to talk anymore. He is too deep in his own thoughts.

The housing is from World War II, white plaster and thin glass. There are bushes and trees surrounding the small huts. Vehicles zoom around the compound. Fences keep the buildings secure. I stagger out of the Jeep and walk toward an empty building.

The door is open. I walk inside. It is cold and damp. There are mattresses on the floors, and I suspect they were used to house new recruits for the militias. Aside from that, the bungalow is bare. An old kitchen is in the back, and a bathroom is around the corner. There is no one else here, so I put one foot outside and wave to Chris. He exits the vehicle, his jacket slung over his shoulder, mud crusted over his black boots.

When Chris shuts the door and we are alone, I feel more tired than I have been in years. I press my back against the wall and close my eyes. I want to sleep for a hundred years, and when I wake up, all of this will be over and everything will be back to normal.

"We'll be okay," Chris says quietly.

He places one hand on each side of the wall above my head, close enough for me to smell his scent – sweat and blood and gunpowder.

"I know," I reply.

I touch his chin and kiss him softly. He pushes his chest against my body and I wrap my arms around his neck, threading my fingers through his dirty-blond hair. He kisses me – a gentle touch at first, but it soon turns desperate and powerful. I slide my hands to his back, fingers brushing over the taught muscles in his shoulders and waist.

I feel hot inside, and suddenly I forget about everything else. My focus becomes one thing: Chris.

I'm not complaining.

I stand on tiptoes as he kisses me, a full foot shorter than him. He hoists me up and I wrap my legs around his waist, boots digging into his belt. He twists around and leans against the wall, his fingers tangling in my hair and his lips on my neck.

"There's nobody else coming in, right?" I ask, breathless, flushed.

"No," he replies. And then he grins. "I locked the door."

"Ah, you devious man." I smile, and he slides down to the floor and I am kissing him again and every other thought and worry goes out the window. He slips his hands down my arms, strips off my jacket and flings it across the room.

"That was in my way," he says, flashing a wry smile.

"Right, right."

I strip off my bulletproof vest. Chris pulls it over my head and slaps it on the floor. Without it, I am twenty pounds lighter and my shoulders feel free. There is a gold chain hanging around my neck, and on the chain there is a small shield. It was a gift from Chris – a Christmas present from long ago.

"You still have it," he murmurs.

"Of course I do. It's my lucky charm."

He kisses the shield.

"It must work," he says, "because you're still here."

"I'm still here," I echo. "With you."

"Yes, with *me*." He pulls me closer and kisses me again, sending shivers down my spine, starting a fire in the pit of my stomach. "And you're not going anywhere else tonight."

"I wouldn't want to," I tell him.

He pulls his shirt off and I place my hand in the center of his warm, muscular chest. There is an ugly scar on his shoulder, where he was once shot during the Battle of the Grapevine. A tattoo of a cobra wraps around one of his biceps. Just under his armpit, near the bottom of his ribcage, there is another tattoo that I haven't noticed before. It's very small.

"What does that say?" I ask, tracing the tiny script with my finger.

"It says 'the shadow of death'," he replies. He leans his head back, his hands behind his head. "Jane was big into religion. She liked the twenty-third psalm. You know. 'Yea, though I walk through the valley of the shadow of death, I will fear no evil, for thou art with me'?"

"I've read it," I reply softly.

"When she died," he goes on, "everything that she believed in – everything that *I* believed in – became a sick joke. I had *the shadow of death* tattooed on my skin to prove my point."

"What *was* your point?" I whisper.

"That no matter what I did, I wasn't safe – and neither were the people I loved." He shrugs. "I thought of it like a curse mark."

"I didn't know you were so superstitious."

"I kept getting screwed over, Cassidy." He shakes his head, clears his throat. "My friends died in combat, my wife got murdered by terrorists. I hated everybody and everything and I just wanted to kill the enemy – every day, as many as I could, as long as I could fight."

I touch his cheek.

"I'm sorry," I say. "I know it was difficult."

He stares at the wall, and for the first time since I have known him, I see the crystal shine of tears in his eyes.

"You changed me," he whispers. "You showed me what it meant to exercise mercy and humanity again. You *saved* me." He pauses. "When I thought you had died on that Coast Guard Cutter, I thought I would die, too. If anything ever happened to you, I told myself that I would find a way to end my life. Go out in a blaze of glory. Kill as many bad guys as I could to avenge your death."

There is a long silence. I hold my breath, he gathers himself, and then he says,

"But I knew that's not what you would have wanted. You would have wanted me to keep fighting. You would have wanted me to keep leading." He holds my face in his hands. "So that's what I did. Cassidy, you've saved my life so many times. I don't deserve you."

A tear slips down my cheek, onto his hand.

"Yes, you do," I say. "We deserve each other."

I kiss him long and hard. He clutches the small of my back and tightens his grip. "I love you," he says.

"You can never say that enough," I laugh. "I love you, too."

He lays me down on my back and kisses my forehead, touches his lips to my neck and traces his mouth all the way to the curve of my collarbone.

"No matter what happens," he says, "this will never change."

I slip my legs around his waist and pull him down to me.

"Never," I say.

It is one of the few things I know to be true.

Chapter Three

Run, don't stop!

I sprint through the trees, drenched in sweat, legs burning, barely able to breathe. The world flashes by in a blur of green and blue. I hold a heavy rifle in my hands, pushing myself harder and harder. I can hear my pursuer, and although I know who it is, I cannot let her catch me.

Not this time.

I keep running until I reach the edge of the forest. A clearing stretches out before me, golden grass waving slightly in the breeze. It is early spring, and the warmth of the sun touches my cheeks as I enter the meadow.

I do not look back. I keep going.

It is only when I reach the other side that I slide to a grinding halt, bringing the rifle up to my shoulder. My pursuer stops and rolls to the ground, crushing the grass. She holds her hands up.

"You're dead," I say. "I've outrun you and outgunned you."

There is an amused smile on my lips. I lower the rifle and pull the bandana off my forehead, sweat dripping down my face. Sophia Rodriguez stands up, and she is panting too hard to reply.

"Nobody," she says between breaths, "can ever take you down in practice."

I sling the rifle over my shoulder, my hands on my knees, inhaling and exhaling.

"You're the fastest," she continues. "You're better than me."

"Chris can catch me," I reply.

"You're always the best," Sophia answers, and the expression on her face looks sad. "Always will be, probably."

I roll my eyes.

"Don't get all weird on me," I say. "It's just war games."

"No," Sophia sighs. "It's actually war."

We have been training every day since Chris and his militia – the Freedom Fighters – rescued us from Omega's slave labor camp. My muscles are stronger than they have ever been. I am learning to move quickly and quietly. I am a good marksman. In fact, my ability to shoot is perhaps my strongest skill set.

"We should go back," Sophia says suddenly. "It's almost chow time."

I look across the clearing. It is so peaceful and quiet here, I almost wish that we could just live here and wait for the apocalypse to end. No more fighting or enslavement or wondering what will happen if Omega finds us.

But I know that is not rational.

I must fight.

I would never forgive myself if I didn't.

*

The sky is clear. The smoke has finally dissipated. The ocean breeze has carried it away, but the visual evidence of the Battle of Monterey is everywhere. Buildings are in ruins. Rubble is scattered across nearly every street.

Omega is gone, but only temporarily.

Our safety here was always an illusion. Smoke and mirrors.

I will never believe in safety again.

I lie with my head on Chris's arm. He is sound asleep, breathing evenly. I trace my finger down the center of his chest, pulling the blanket tighter around myself.

It is a cold morning, but Chris is keeping me warm.

I smile at the ceiling, sit up, and smooth my hair. Not that it helps.

I head toward the bathroom. I briefly shower in cold water, pull on my spare uniform and peer at my reflection in the cracked mirror over the sink. The edge of my right eye is black and blue, and my bottom lip is split. My cheek is bruised. There are gashes on the side of my neck where Sophia dug her fingernails into my skin during our fight.

I drop my gaze and stare at the grimy sink.

Don't think about her any more, I tell myself. *She made her choice and you made yours.*

I know that this is true, but the reality of her death still stings.

It hurts because she did not die side by side with me in battle.

She died as my enemy, and that will haunt me forever.

I open the bathroom door and step into the bungalow. Chris is sitting on the mattress. He looks at me as I emerge, smiling crookedly.

"Sleep well?" he teases.

I blush and sit beside him.

"You would know," I reply.

He takes my hand, kisses it, and holds it against his knee.

"We're outnumbered," he says at last. "All of this fighting...all of this backbreaking to get into the Alliance...and we're still outnumbered. Omega will keep coming. They won't stop. If what Harry said is true – if Omega has infiltrated every level of society in the country – what can we do to stop it?"

"Why would you say that?" I demand, afraid. "You're the one who's always believed that we can win this war. More than me, even! You've always had hope. Don't say stuff like that."

"I'm stating facts, Cassie," Chris replies, raising an eyebrow. "This is not a fair fight. We're fighting for our lives. Omega is just fighting for a foothold."

"So we're motivated," I say and shrug. "We've got more incentive than they do."

Chris shakes his head.

"We could be fooling ourselves. This could be the end."

I look at him. Words form in my mouth, but I can't force them past my lips. Chris has always been the leader of this movement – the one who has believed that no matter what, we will win. I don't know why he would say this. While the facts might be correct, I refuse to believe that we will lose this war.

We just *can't*.

"I won't give up," I tell him. "I will *never* stop fighting."

Chris smiles, but there is sadness in his eyes.

"Neither will I," he agrees. "Fight or die, right?"

I mock fist-bump his hand.

"Right," I say.

"What do we do with Harry?" I ask quietly. "I know I asked you earlier, but still...what's our timeline with him?"

"We interrogate him," Chris replies, without hesitation. "And then we kill him."

I nod.

If anyone deserves death, it is Harry Lydell.

But then I think of all the blood on my hands and I wonder: am I really so different than my enemy?

Yes, I tell myself. *I am not an aggressor. I am a defender. There is a difference.*

But that will never change the fact that I have taken lives. I will have to live with that for the rest of my life...however long that may be.

I miss the old world, but deep down, I know that we will never be the same. Society will never be rebuilt. We are doomed to a new civilization of post-apocalyptic survivors deprived of technology and organized government.

We must repeat our own history in order to live again.

We must die, so that we can be reborn.

*

We leave the bungalow and enter the clear, crisp morning. The sunshine is a much-welcomed warmth on my face. I savor it before we step into the chow hall. It is an old building with tables and chairs. When we walk in, militia soldiers stop and stare: first at Chris, then at me.

Whatever, I think. *I don't care.*

I walk to the food line – a long bar of buffet food – and shovel items onto my plate. It smells good inside, like scrambled eggs and bacon. Chris follows. We fill our mugs with steaming cups of coffee and take a seat in the corner, near the open windows.

Manny walks in with Elle a few moments later.

"I'm going to talk to Manny for a second, hang tight," Chris excuses himself, then walks over to the crazy pilot, discussing something about flying overwatch and last night's battle. Elle stands silently beside him, listening to every word, her dog close beside her, silent and pensive.

Vera enters the building and offers a weak smile to Chris.

He says something to her and she replies. They begin talking and I roll my eyes, reminded of a similar scene not so long ago in the mountains – in a cafeteria, even. I used to sit at a table and watch Chris and Vera talk while I huddled up with Sophia, talking about Chris and the war and whether or not we were going to survive life in the militias...

Sophia, why did you have to betray us all?

But now I am a new girl. I am a woman, I guess. I am a leader.

I am struck with the knowledge that while I will never be beautiful like Vera, I will always be honest, and I will always be the one who is willing to lay down her life if it is asked of her.

I look over at Chris. He finishes speaking with Vera, and she and I exchange a look. She nods, a half smile on her face, and I nod back. Chris sits beside me and touches my shoulder.

"You seem deep in thought," he says.

"I was just analyzing the meaning of my life," I reply.

"Do share."

"I'm not Marilyn Monroe but I'm a good shot and I pack mean left hook."

Chris gives me a puzzled look.

"What's *that* supposed to mean?" he asks.

"I don't know," I reply. "Maybe it just means that I'm finally okay with who I am. With who I've become."

Chris shrugs. "Yeah? Well, I've *always* been okay with it."

I crack a wry grin.

"Why?" I ask.

"Why am I okay with your good aim and left hook?" he says.

"No!" I laugh. "Why are you okay with who I am? Who I *was*?"

Chris softly touches my hair, a boyish, demure expression on his face.

"Cassidy, you're an amazing woman. I love you – everything about you."

"But why?"

He raises an eyebrow.

"Is this some kind of test that women make guys go through?"

"Consider this your final exam." I smirk.

Chris shakes his head, but he finally answers.

"I don't know, Cassie," he says. "You're just...real." He places his hand on the small of my back, and I feel warmth spread through my chest. "You're mine, and I love you for that."

The breeze picks up, combing its cool, invisible fingers through my hair.

"I used to hate who I was," I say quietly. "I was never good enough for myself." I smile. "It's like the apocalypse showed me what life was all about, you know? I became stronger. It changed me, but I'm glad it did."

Chris kisses the side of my cheek.

"Honestly, I liked the innocent, naïve side of you," Chris answers, "but I like this side of you, too. Like I said, I love you for all of it."

The sunrise touches the edge of the city.

"I love you, too," I say. "For all of it."

*

The Naval Postgraduate School is no longer safe, so we meet in an old warehouse near Cannery Row. The tourist strip has been reduced to little more than twisted metal and smoldering piles of wreckage. It is sad to see it so ravaged, but that is what happens in war. Things get broken.

The warehouse is wide and cold. I stand near Chris. He keeps his arm around me as I button my dark jacket. Vera walks in. She has cleaned up, as have the rest of my friends. Uriah's black hair is combed, slick and shiny. Elle enters with Bravo, and right behind her is Manny, clad in a leather jacket, his wild gray hair flying in all directions. But his expression is sober. He keeps one hand on Elle's shoulder – she is his niece, and he has been very protective of her since their reunion just two days ago.

"There are reports," Chris begins once everyone has gathered, "that Omega has a naval fleet of a hundred thousand men loitering offshore of the California coast."

Anita Vega walks in through the door, flanked by guards.

"Those are not just reports or rumors," she announces. "They are true. The Air Force has seen the ships. Omega is sending more."

My heart drops to my stomach. I feel like the *Titanic*, hitting an iceberg and sinking to the bottom of the sea.

"So what we have here, ladies and gentlemen," Manny says, "is an unstoppable wave of soldiers from around the world who are not only better armed than we are, but more organized, if only because they possess modern technology and we're still using two tin cans and a piece of string."

"We need more recruits," I reply.

"It's more than that, Commander Hart," Anita interjects. "We need more weapons, more fighter jets, more naval vessels. We need nuclear bombs. We need to retaliate. Omega is attempting a total takeover of the North American and South American continents. They must be destroyed, and if the only way to eliminate them is by using an atomic bomb...then so be it."

"Easy now," Manny retorts. "You're talking about starting a nuclear war. Notice that Omega hasn't let any of their atomic bombs loose on us. Why? Because they want to use North America for something. They can't do that if it's steeped in radiation. That throws a wrench in their plans."

"They are going to *kill us all*," Vera hisses. "Don't you see that? They have invaded our country, they're killing our people, and they're taking over. It's *time* for extreme measures."

"Whoa," I reply, holding my hand up. "First of all, we don't have any nuclear bombs at our disposal that *I* know of. And second of all, even if we did, who would we bomb? Omega is everywhere. They're here. We can't just bomb ourselves."

"Start with China," Vera states. "They're the ones supplying the foot soldiers."

"And then what? They nuke us back? Do you really want that, Vera?"

"I want them to pay." She fists her hands. "Don't *you*?"

"Of course I want them to *pay*," I reply. "But I'd like to preserve our home in the process. That's the whole point of this war – to protect and preserve, remember?"

The warehouse is wide and empty, and our voices echo off the walls.

"This isn't about revenge," Uriah says. "This is about survival."

"Well, half of the council for the Pacific Northwest Alliance is dead," Anita tells us, "either by assassination or in the Battle of Monterey. We are what's left. All of us, the decision is ours. The Air Force and the National Guard is looking to us for a decision."

The burden of that leadership weighs heavy on me. I feel like I can hardly breathe beneath the weight of it. The militia leaders – some of which are also senators, like myself – are the only remaining strong leadership on the west coast.

"What about the Senate in Sacramento?" I ask. "We have leadership there."

"Hardly," Devin says. He is standing in the back of the room – I hadn't even noticed him walk in. "After the bombing on the Capitol, more than seventy percent of the Senate was wiped out. That was Omega's intention – decapitate the leadership we created."

"So it's all on us now," Vera replies.

"Correct."

She curses under her breath.

I look at Chris, then I walk to a plastic table near the edge of the wall and pick up a stack of papers. "Do you know what these are?" I ask.

Everyone but Chris gives me a blank look.

"This is a list of the dead," I answer. "The men and women that died in the Battle of Monterey."

Silence.

"We need more recruits," Chris picks up. "The militias are strong, but Omega is outnumbering us. Again. We've got to have more fighters."

"Where are we going to get fighters from?" Anita demands. "I brought *everyone* from Mexico with me! The other militia groups are defending our coastline from further Omega invasion."

"We're spread too thin," Uriah observes. "Like too little butter on toast."

"Thank you for the analogy, Lieutenant True." Anita rolls her eyes. "My point is – we have no way of contacting the rest of the country, and the west coast is already spent. We have nothing left to give. There are no more recruits to *be* recruited."

I think of my days spent in the mountains, with the Mountain Rangers and Freedom Fighters. Our soldiers were salt of the earth people, former lawyers and schoolteachers and shop owners. They were not born fighters – they were *made* fighters. They were the survivors of the apocalypse.

So who is left to fight? Our supply of recruits is finite.

No, I think. *There has to be more people. The Midwest? The East Coast?*

I catch Chris's eye.

What do we do? I think. *What's the next step?*

"Ladies and gentlemen," Manny interrupts, holding his hands up. "I hate to interrupt this highly intellectual argument; er, *conversation.* But I just got a radio message that we've got some important visitors arriving outside."

We gather at the doorway, and in the distance, I see a helicopter slowly moving toward us. My defenses kick in and I tense.

"Omega messengers?" Uriah says.

"No," Chris replies. "That's not an Omega chopper."

There is a landing strip that the militias have created – it is a strip of Highway 152, a long slab of concrete.

The helicopter is black. I can hear the steady beat that it makes as it slices through the air. There is a strange insignia painted on the side of the chopper – a green circle with a tree in the center.

"I've never seen that symbol before," I say.

"Neither have I," Vera agrees.

"It could be another militia," Anita suggests.

I exchange glances with Chris.

"I don't think so," he says.

We watch as it lands in the distance.

I step out the door.

I want to be the first to find out who it is.

*

"Don't even think about it," I joke, laughing. I lift my bowl of stew high above my head, trying to escape Chris's reach. He grabs it and holds it over his head now, chuckling heartily.

Andrew and Derek make a snide comment and several people near the campfire erupt into laughter. Chris grins and gives me the bowl. I playfully smack his arm, taking a seat on a blanket in the dirt.

We have been camping here for a few months now. My muscles are no longer sore from the war games. My aim is excellent. I have survived several ambushes and, for the first time in my life, I am confident that I am good at what I do.

"You've got short people problems," Chris says, draping his arm behind my back, kissing the side of my cheek.

"Yeah, you've got tall people problems," I remark. "Too bad, so sad."

"Get a room, people, geez," Derek snickers.

I toss a small rock at him. He catches it neatly in the palm of his hand.

"Nice one, Hart."

I finish my stew. Chris is talking to Andrew. Mrs. Young is combing out Isabel's long, unruly blonde hair. Jeff comes to the fire, his looks just as striking and handsome as his older brother's. He joins in on the conversation.

Near the edge of camp, in the shadows, I see Harry. He is staring at everyone, a sour expression on his face. He is completely alone, as always, and I feel a stab of guilt.

When I am done eating, I stand up and cross the campsite, heading his way. When he sees me, he drops his gaze to the ground and pretends to concentrate on his stew.

"Do you enjoy being a loner?" I ask.

"Ah, Cassidy," he replies. "Always so sarcastic."

"You don't have to be isolated forever," I tell him. "I've forgiven you for what you've done. You can be a part of this place now."

"You've forgiven me?" Harry laughs. "But no one else has."

"I've got a big heart." I tap my chest and take a seat on the log beside him. The firelight sends flickering shadows across the trees. "Seriously. I'm trying to be nice to you here, Harry. Throw me a bone, will you?"

Harry sets his bowl on the ground, folding his hands together.

"This is a lie," he says quietly.

"Come again?"

"This. Militias, fighting, training. Rebellion." He rolls his eyes. "It's a waste of time. Omega will win, in the end, and we'll all be dead. Why fight?"

"Because some people actually have a spine," I reply.

"Are you quite certain that you've completely forgiven me, Cassie?" he says, an amused smile on his face.

"Don't call me Cassie," I mutter.

He raises his eyebrows, but says nothing.

"This militia could be your second chance," I say. "You're lucky."

Harry snorts. He turns to me, then, watching my hair blowing in the breeze.

"You're so blindly loyal," he whispers. "Why?"

"Loyal, yes," I reply. "Blind, no. I know exactly what I'm doing."

"Do you?" Harry shakes his head. "There's always an easier way."

"And what is your solution to the apocalypse?"

Harry doesn't answer. He just reaches out, touches the hair on my forehead and pushes it backward, slowly. I stare at him as he does this. He pulls his hand back.

"I wish you could see the look on your face," he smiles.

Although meant to be kind, I can't help but think that his smile comes across as a little predatory. Spiteful. This man did send me to my death in order to save his own life, after all.

"You're wrong," I say.

"About what?"

"Everything. The way you think. You're just wrong." I stand up. "In the end, Harry, when it's dark and cold, I want to die surrounded by my friends." I break my gaze. "Think about that."

I walk away, but as I head back toward Chris, Jeff and the others, Harry replies, "It's too late for me now."

I am afraid to ask him what he means.

Chapter Four

The helicopter lands on the strip. Chris and I stand next to each other, the wind whipping the orange flags along the freeway divider into circles.

The units on the landing strip roll into place, Humvees and trucks. Militia soldiers stand around the chopper, armed.

"You!" I say, talking to a soldier with red hair. I remember him, glance at his nametag, and say, "O'Byrne."

He snaps around and looks at me, saluting. There is a tiny smile on his face.

"Yes, Commander?"

"What's the deal with this chopper, soldier? Who is it?"

"We don't know, ma'am," he replies. "They've radioed in. They said they bring help and that they're supporting the militias."

I look at Chris.

"Who gave them clearance to land?" he asks.

"The Air Force, I guess," O'Byrne replies.

The chopper doors open, and the militia guards – all thirty of them – train their weapons on the chopper. I watch carefully, observing every detail. A woman steps out, coifed gray hair and belted brown combat fatigues.

Recognition hits me like a lightning bolt.

"Arlene?" I say.

She steps down off the chopper, locking eyes with me first, and then her eyes fall to Manny and Elle.

"Oh, my God," she says, touching her fingers to her lips. She rushes forward, and then Manny has taken her in his arms, embracing her. Elle looks shocked as the woman embraces her, too, and they all talk to each other, just out of earshot.

"Cassidy," Chris whispers. "Who's Arlene?"

"She's..." I smile suddenly. "I guess you weren't there, were you? She ran the Way House in the Tehachapi Mountains. She gave us horses for Operation Angel Pursuit when I took a team into Los Angeles to rescue you."

"Ah, the Way House that had been attacked?" Chris looks grim. "Good to know that she survived."

I nod. Manny turns to us.

"Ladies and gentlemen," he says. "I'd like you to meet my wife."

*

"Why didn't you tell me you were *married*?" I demand, laughing.

"You didn't ask," Manny offers, keeping one arm draped around Arlene's shoulders. I embrace her. She has deep wrinkles around her eyes, and at a glance, she almost looks like she could pass as Manny's sister, rather than his wife.

"What happened?" I ask.

"It's a long story," she replies. "Please, meet my pilot, Alan."

A tall, sinewy bald man climbs out of the chopper, tossing a headset back into the pilot's seat. He strides over, and I notice that he has one lazy eye.

"Pleased to meet you," he says.

His voice has a distinctly Irish accent.

"Lieutenant Alan White," Arlene says. "This is Commander Cassidy Hart and Commander Chris Young." She smiles at Chris. "I'm glad to see that Operation Angel Pursuit was a success. I'm sorry I couldn't congratulate you in person when everything happened."

"You have nothing to apologize for," I say.

She lifts her shoulders, her lips turning upward.

"You have survived the Battle of Monterey," she sighs. "God, things haven't gotten any easier in the past two months, have they?"

I shake my head.

"I have important information from the Underground," she tells Chris, looking straight at him. "Where can we talk where it's safe?"

"This way," he replies, gesturing to a Humvee.

Manny, Arlene and Elle get into the back seat. Bravo sits at their feet, ever silent and obedient. I sit in the center seat up front, and Lieutenant Alan White, the pilot, sits beside me.

"Sorry, it's a bit of a squeeze," he apologizes.

"No worries," I assure him.

44

He smells heavily of cigarette smoke, and I notice a pack stuck in his jacket pocket. "How long was the flight, Lieutenant White?" I ask.

He hesitates, then Arlene says, "We'll tell you everything once we get to a safe place."

I don't question her. I understand the need for secrecy.

There are spies everywhere.

We roll through several checkpoints before we reach the warehouse again. It is a silent ride, and then we exit the vehicle, heading through the guarded doors. Anita Vega and the others are waiting for us when we return.

"Arlene Costas," I say. "This is Anita Vega and Devin May. You've already met Vera."

Vera doesn't smile, but she does look surprised to see Arlene.

"Yes," Arlene replies. "You're missing Derek and Andrew."

"Andrew was wounded. Derek is in Sacramento."

"I see. You're certain there are no listening devices in this building?" she asks, looking at the high windows.

"Everything's been checked," I tell her.

"Seal the rooms," she tells me.

Chris gives the command, and the guards leave the room. They shut the door and we are left in total privacy.

"I'm sorry for the theatrics," Arlene says, "but what I have to say to you is beyond secret. It's of the utmost importance that Omega never finds out."

Anita frowns and takes a seat on a plastic chair. Arlene pats Elle's shoulder and walks to the back of the room, looking at the table with the lists of dead.

"I come from a top secret Underground location known as Sky City," she tells us. "Lieutenant White is our best pilot—"

"Aside from myself, of course," Manny interrupts.

"Of course, dear." Arlene pretends to be irritated with him, but I see nothing but affection on her face. "As I was saying, Lieutenant White and myself come from Sky City. At this point in time, it is the most secure Underground base on the entire West Coast – possibly the entire country." She folds her arms across her chest. "I escaped to Halo Point, right after Omega raided my safe house in the Tehachapi Mountains. After it became too dangerous to stay at Halo Point, I was relocated to Sky City."

"Sky City," Anita states. "I've heard of it. I thought it was just a rumor."

I look around the room, confused.

"Where is Sky City?" I ask.

"The high mountains," Arlene replies. "*Very* high. We are beyond the trees, in the snow. Most of our facility is based completely under the ground, invisible from satellites and Omega observation. We are burrowed deep into the side of a volcanic mountain, in the clouds."

"How is that possible?" Vera wonders. "How did you build an underground base in the high mountains?"

Arlene takes a deep breath.

"Sky City is part of an organization known as *Unite*," she explains. "They are an off-branch of what people once considered to be paranoid doomsday prepper organizations. Only their work was funded by the Federal Government."

"Omega had infected every level of government before the EMP, according to Harry Lydell," I tell her. "How do you know Omega doesn't already know about this?"

"Because I've helped build it," Arlene answers. "*Unite* was originally created during World War Two, when everyone was afraid that the Nazis were going to get the atomic bomb first." She shrugs. "Obviously they didn't, but our facilities were already built by that point. Sky City has only gotten bigger since then. I have been helping Unite these last three decades, and our top priority has always been secrecy."

"Is it a safe haven?" Chris asks. "Do you shelter survivors?"

"No," she says. "We make soldiers."

Anita inhales sharply.

"How many men do you have?"

"Three thousand," she replies.

I bite my lip.

Omega has millions. We are still outnumbered.

"I began working for *Unite* when I was just twenty years old," she says. "We have grown from a small facility to a massive underground network. We are, in essence, exactly what our name says: a *city*. We in Sky City have been anticipating an invasion like this for years. We've always known about Omega, and we've been preparing for it."

"You knew about Omega?" Vera asks. "You knew the EMP was coming? Why didn't you warn people? Why didn't the government say anything? Why didn't the media—"

"Because Omega was too deep into the government," Arlene says. "There was nothing we could do. To reveal ourselves to the public or to *anyone* would have meant exposing ourselves to the enemy and therefore compromising our security. Because we played it smart, we are still intact. We can offer hope."

Chris sits down on a chair, leaning his forearms on his knees.

"Why did they send you here?" he asks Arlene.

"Sky City is the epicenter for all Underground operations," she replies. "It has been since the beginning. The militia movement was organic, but we have always been in the background, helping recruit, helping guide the remains of the United States Military forces. Some of the brightest and most brilliant minds are in Sky City."

"So why are you here?" I ask, echoing Chris's earlier question. "Why leave the safety of such a secure facility and risk exposure to come to Monterey, when Omega is getting ready to send a hundred thousand foot soldiers into the West Coast?"

Arlene smiles.

"We want to help," she says. "We've been working in the background for a long time, but we'd like to offer our recruits to the militias. Our soldiers are some of the most highly trained units in the world. They are skilled in guerilla warfare and they know more about Omega than anyone else. We may not have a hundred thousand men, but we are just as strong."

I take a seat beside Chris, overwhelmed by this information.

"We'll take all the help we can get," Chris says at last. "We need more recruits – now more than ever."

"Good." Arlene looks at Manny, and then she looks at me. "However, there *is* a catch."

I knew it. Nothing this good could be free.

"Our recruits are somewhat hesitant to leave Sky City," she says. "Some of them don't believe that it's the right time. They think we should wait for a more opportune moment." She shakes her head. "They don't understand that the opportune moment is *now*. We need someone from the front lines to speak with our Commander and convince him that now is the time to move."

"Who is your Commander?" Chris asks.

"It would be wiser if I didn't give you his name," she replies. "But he's known as *Freebird* on the Underground radio waves."

"So you want one of us to come to Sky City and convince your Commander to give the green light," I say. "Sounds fair."

"I don't know about you," Manny replies, "but I'm beginning to think that Sky City sounds a little too good to be true."

Arlene snorts.

"You'll see," she says, lifting her head. "You'll all see." She looks at us. "So which one of you is going to Sky City with me?"

No one answers.

Somehow, I know before anyone says a word that it is going to be me.

*

"I can't go with you," Chris says.

We are standing near the tide pools in the curve of the Monterey Peninsula. The air is sharp and cold, but it heightens my senses and keeps me alert. The ocean beats against the rocks, sending sprays of water in every direction. Seagulls fly over our heads and crabs scuttle through the shallower pools.

"I know," I tell him.

I knew this. I knew that when I told Arlene that I would go to Sky City to talk to the Commander there, I would be alone. Chris cannot abandon Monterey. He must protect it until I can come back with more troops.

"Why?" Chris asks.

"Why *what*?"

"Why does it have to be you? *Every* time?"

I shake my head.

"I don't know," I say. "I don't ask for this stuff."

"You just volunteer for it."

"You would do the same thing." I fold my arms across my chest. "Don't tell me you wouldn't. Because that's a lie."

Chris looks at me long and hard, then drops his gaze.

"I would," he says. "If you weren't here."

I close my eyes.

"I'm sorry," I reply. "But this is the right thing to do. I know it is."

"Your instinct is usually right." He grins half-heartedly. "There's a reason people listen to you, you know. It's because you're believable. You're real. You don't pretend to be something you're not, and people can relate to you. They like seeing an honest fighter."

"Apparently." I sit down on a splintered, wooden bench. He joins me. The steady rhythm of the ocean waves beating the rocks is soothing. "Listen, Chris. I love you. Me doing this has nothing to do with me *not* loving you. I'm doing this because I think it will help *all* of us."

"I know it will." Chris puts his arm behind me, draping it across the bench. "I just wish we could go together." He kisses the side of my head. "I don't like being separated. Things change so fast, staying together has always been our best shot at surviving this war."

"I know that, too," I say quietly. "But I have to do this."

"Yes," Chris says after a long pause. "You do."

I lean my head against his shoulder and hold his hand. The sun sinks slowly into the distant horizon, burnt orange and then blood red.

"You know," I whisper, "I always loved going to the beach when I was growing up. My mom used to take me all the time. It was our favorite thing. We'd put our feet in the water, lie in the sun for a few hours, bring a picnic. It was so nice. No worries at all."

Chris smiles against my hair.

"And I used to surf in every wave up and down the coast." He laughs. "After Jane died, I lived in the water. It saved my life."

There is an awkward pause after he mentions his deceased wife's name, but I relax into the silence. The past is the past, and Chris's marriage to Jane is part of what makes him who he is today – the man that I love *now*. And I guess I should be thankful to her for that.

"The end of the world brought us together," Chris says at last. "But it won't tear us apart."

I smile.

No. Regardless of what happens, it never will.

Chapter Five

I'm nervous. I look at the small plane on the freeway-turned-tarmac and try to loosen the knot in my stomach. There are guards everywhere. Above my head, an American flag snaps in the sharp ocean breeze. I've got my duffel bag over my shoulder, my rifle across my back and my Beretta handgun strapped to my hip. My mouth is dry.

"Cassidy."

Chris stands beside me, pressing something into my hand. My fingers close around the smooth handle of a knife. *My* knife. My name is carved into the handle, a gift from Chris's brother Jeff, killed in action months ago.

"Where did you find it?" I ask, shocked.

"I forgot to give it to you earlier. Harry had it on him when we brought him in."

I nod. Of course. Harry took it from me several days ago.

I'm glad I have it back.

"Thank you," I say.

Chris pulls a piece of paper from his jacket pocket and hands it to me.

"What are you, the giving tree?" I smirk. "What's this?"

"Mission roster," he replies.

"Ah." I hold it out, reading the names.

Manny Costas

Arlene Costas

Vera Wright

Uriah True

Elle Costas – K9 Unit

"You're sending the whole team with me?" I ask. "You can't do that."

"I didn't do it," he replies. "They volunteered. They love you, Cassie. They want to make sure you come back safe – plus they want this Sky City thing to work out for us. We need the recruits, and if Arlene is right, this could be a pivotal move for the Alliance."

"What about Andrew?" I ask. "Is he going to be okay?"

"Andrew is fine. By the time you're back, he'll be operational." Chris flashes a sad smile, touching my cheek. "I love you, Cassie. Don't do anything stupid."

"Please," I reply, rolling my eyes. "I haven't done anything stupid in *at least* three days."

I wrap my arms around his neck and he folds me into a strong hug.

"I love you, too," I whisper.

He kisses me, and his touch is warm and wonderful and it makes me ache, knowing that I will be separated from him again. I don't want this. I don't want *any* of this. But none of the heartbreak will end unless we defeat Omega, so this is my fate.

I kiss him one last time, drawing my thumb over his whiskery cheek.

"Stay safe, Chris," I say.

Tears burn like acid in the back of my throat. This hurts.

To me, this is more painful than being shot. And I have the experience to make the comparison. I blink back the tears, stuff the mission roster into my pocket, strap the knife to my belt, and touch Chris's hand one last time.

"Good luck, Commander," he says softly.

I accept his farewell with a tip of my head, and then I am walking across the tarmac, not daring to look back. Because if I look back, I know I will cry, and I cannot allow that. I keep my eyes on Vera. She is standing near the front of the plane, hair slicked back into a tight ponytail, expression steely.

"Vera," I say quietly.

"Commander." She folds her arms. "You're doing the right thing."

"Yeah," I reply. "I know."

"And Cassidy?"

I wait.

"I'm sorry," she says. "About what happened with Sophia."

I force myself to remain stoic.

"So am I," I tell her.

I look at the plane. The door is open, and there is a narrow staircase leading inside. I can see Uriah walking toward us. Arlene stands at the top of the staircase, dressed in dark fatigues and a loose jacket. She looks calm and serene, her gray hair knotted on top of her head in a loose bun.

"Are you ready, Commander?" she asks me.

"How long will it take to get there?" I say.

"Not long."

Great. I love the detailed answers.

"With me flying," Manny says, descending the staircase, his gray hair in a ridiculous tumult, "we'll get there in no time at all." He winks at me. "That is, of course, if we don't go sightseeing along the way."

"Oh, Manny stop," Arlene tells him, but there is a smile on her face. "We all know you're the best pilot."

"Ah, except for *Alan White*." He rolls his eyes. "Apparently he's the *new* breed of pilot."

"Once a pilot, always a pilot, my love," Arlene grins, disappearing into the maw of the plane.

"She's obsessed with me," Manny shrugs. "She married me for my charm and good looks, as you can plainly see." He wiggles his eyebrows, forcing a weak smile out of me. "Ah, a smile. That's the Cassidy Hart I know."

Vera makes a face.

"I can't take all the sentimentality," she says.

She walks up the staircase in a huff, which only makes me smile wider.

"Thank you for flying us, Manny," I say.

"My pleasure, as always."

I hug him briefly and put one foot on the stairs. I pause, look behind my shoulder, and see Chris at the end of the tarmac. He is standing there, watching me, a sad expression on his face.

Don't look back, I think to myself. *Don't do that to yourself.*

I take a deep breath, climb the stairs, and then I am inside the plane.

I am as good as gone.

*

When I am asleep, I dream of happier days. I see myself with my mother and father – before their divorce – walking down the streets of a busy Los Angeles boulevard. I see myself reading a book in the window seat on a rainy day. I see myself making dinner for my father on a Saturday night, and reading the newspaper on a lazy Sunday morning.

Before the divorce, my mother would make a pot of coffee on Sundays, turn on the television and watch whatever romantic comedy was on. She would sit there in her pajamas, a pensive expression on her face.

"Cassidy," she'd say. "I want more for you. I want you to really be able to take care of yourself. I don't want you to be dependent on anybody – not even me."

Growing up, it was the one thing that my mother said that I took to heart.

The rest of it was, in my mind, irrelevant. She left me, she moved away, and therefore she was the enemy. I barely saw her. She was the manager of a hotel – or so she'd told me. Whether or not that was true was up for debate.

Dad and I never talked about her, I was alone with my thoughts on that one.

"If anything ever happens to me," Dad would say, "Mom will take care of you."

In my heart, I knew that wasn't true.

I would always have to take care of myself.

It was my fate.

It still is.

*

Something shoves me. I wake up, hitting the floor on my shoulder. My heart rate skyrockets and a burst of adrenaline fires through my system. The small cabin of the little plane is shaking badly. Uriah comes up behind me and pulls me to my feet, his strong arms steadying me.

"It's okay," he tells me. "It's just turbulence, according to Manny."

I look at my seat, still shaky and breathing hard.

"Okay," I reply. "I'm okay."

I touch Uriah's hands.

"You can let go of me, Uriah," I say.

"Oh, yeah." He steps back, still watching me closely. "Sorry."

I sit down in the chair. The cabin is painted in muted blue and white tones. It reminds me of a hospital, and I don't like it. Elle Costas is sitting at the front of the cabin, silent in her seat, stroking Bravo's fur. Behind me, Vera is staring out the window.

"Don't worry!" Manny calls from the pilot's cockpit. "I've got it all under control. If we're about to die, I'll be the first to tell you!"

"Freaking maniac," Vera mutters under her breath.

Despite my racing heart, I laugh a little.

Uriah sits down in the seat across the aisle. His dark hair is combed back, and I notice that he's got a scar on the left side of his neck.

"How'd that happen?" I ask, touching my neck.

"I don't even remember anymore," he says.

I look out the window. The Central Valley is a tiny blur of yellow and green beneath us. Clouds wisp by outside, and up here, suspended in the air, I feel immune to Omega's effects. I can understand why Manny loves flying so much.

It is freeing.

"Do you really think this is going to change the way things are going?" Uriah asks suddenly.

"Yes," I say.

"Three thousand troops," Uriah goes on. "That's nothing against Omega."

I look him in the eye.

"We have to try," I tell him. "It's the best we can do."

"But Omega will come back with millions."

"They've *been* coming at us with millions," I say. "But we've been pushing them back every time. We just have to pray to God that Chris and the Alliance can hold

Monterey's defenses together long enough to keep Omega from charging up the West Coast again."

Uriah folds his long, slender fingers together.

"And if our defenses don't hold?" he says.

"Then we stand," I conclude. "And we deal."

A smile spreads across his lips.

"You," he says, "are the strongest person I know."

I turn my gaze to the window.

"Not by a long shot," I answer.

"Hey, passengers," Manny says, walking into the hall.

"Um, hello, *pilot*," Vera nearly yells. "Shouldn't you be *flying* the plane?"

"Arlene has taken over for a moment," he replies. "She's not as good as me, of course, but she'll do." He laughs at his own joke. "The turbulence is over for the time being. Enjoying the flight?"

I lift my shoulders.

"Ah, I see." He strolls over to Elle and ruffles her hair. "Elle, don't be so asocial. Come join the party. Uriah and Cassidy are nearly getting ready to pop open the champagne bottles."

Elle slowly stands up and sits closer, never saying a word.

She doesn't look to be in the partying mood.

That makes two of us.

"Why all the somber faces?" Manny asks. "Life isn't that bad, is it?"

No one answers.

"Well," he sighs. "Apparently I've been outvoted. If anyone is interested, we should be there in about an hour. Hang tight, ladies and gentlemen. Manny will get you there safe and sound. I hope."

He laughs again and saunters back to the cockpit.

"Has he always been this crazy?" Vera asks Elle.

Elle shrugs.

"As far as I know," she replies.

"Figures." Vera settles back into her seat. "We're all crazy."

I don't disagree.

Chapter Six

I look out the window. The crystalline blue gray peaks of the high Sierra Nevada Mountains glimmer in the sunshine below. The caps are tipped with powdery snow. The Kings River carves a deep wrinkle through the canyon. Patches of green and brown smear the canvas of the mountain range. It is beautiful. It is huge.

"We're here," Uriah whispers.

A gorgeous collection of smaller peaks surround an icy lake, similar in size and shape to a pothole. Manny circles the lake several times, getting lower and lower. Trees are sparser up here. The higher elevation means less oxygen, and less tree growth.

"Where's the airstrip?" Elle asks, leaning forward.

"Who knows?" Vera says.

"I'm glad we all trust Manny completely," I comment.

Vera huffs.

As we get closer to the ground, I see that a strip of earth has been cleared away next to the lake, smooth and long. It is a landing strip, and it is nearly impossible to see from the air.

The plane slowly descends, and I can hear Manny hooting and hollering from the cockpit – and Arlene's terse responses.

We dip forward as the front wheels touch the ground. The plane lands, and we are coasting down the small airstrip. We slow down quickly. I unbuckle my seatbelt and stand up.

"Let me do the talking," Arlene says, stepping out of the cockpit.

I raise an eyebrow.

"I thought you brought me here to talk," I reply.

"Well...yes. But still. At first." She touches my shoulder. "Trust me, Commander."

I make no promises.

The door on the plane opens. Manny finishes up in the cockpit and steps into the narrow hall. "See? I got us here in one piece, didn't I?"

"Thank God," Arlene murmurs.

As the door opens, I feel a rush of freezing cold air. I brace myself. Clear, unfiltered sunlight hits my face. Manny and Uriah pull out the staircase. I look outside, seeing some figures on the tarmac.

"Friends of yours?" I ask Arlene.

"Allies, yes," she replies.

She steps outside, descending the staircase. I share a sideways glance with Vera and Uriah – they return it. I don't have to say anything to them to communicate the fact that we should not let our guard down. Not for a second.

I follow her.

There is snow everywhere. The small, icy lake sits in the middle of a ring of sharp, jagged rock formations.

The air is thin, and I can smell the damp mountain soil. Wet, thick clouds swirl around the tips of the rocky peaks.

I walk down the staircase. There are no trees. Everything is rocky and barren, cold and deserted. The figures standing near the edge of the tarmac are dressed in light-colored fatigues. Guards. They are well armed. About ten of them, male and female.

In the middle of the guards, a tall, burly man stands with a cigar wedged between his teeth. I freeze, staring.

No. No way. Please tell me I'm imagining this.

"Colonel Rivera?" I say.

He taps the ashes of his cigar on his finger. His dark, angry eyes say everything I need to know.

"You're involved with this?" I demand, storming forward. "What are you *doing* here, Colonel?"

I have not seen this man since the bombing of the Capitol Building in Sacramento. I do not like him. I never have. I probably never will.

"Arlene?" Vera says, folding her arms.

Arlene gives me a weak smile.

"I'm sorry," she replies. "Colonel Rivera has been a part of the Sky City operation for a long time. After the incident in Sacramento, he was relocated here, with me."

I stare at him.

So *this* is the man I was sent to convince to send us backup?

The man who *denied* backup to the militias during the Battle of the Grapevine?

The man who left Chris to die at the hands of Harry Lydell and Omega?

I am red with rage. Infuriated that Arlene kept this little bit information from me. I turn to her, and I know she can see the fury in my expression. She swallows. But I can tell by Manny and Elle's reactions that they are just as surprised as I am to see the Colonel.

Arlene hadn't told them, either.

"What's the matter, Colonel?" Manny says. "Has it been so long that you don't remember our names anymore?"

"Welcome to Sky City," he says. His voice is tight, controlled. "Commander Hart, Lieutenant Wright, Lieutenant True. Manny Costas." He jams the cigar between his teeth. "I trust your flight in was enjoyable?"

He looks directly at me when he says this.

"You know why we're here." I briefly salute him, determined to keep this professional. I will *not* explode.

I turn to Arlene and say, "He *does* know, right?"

She nods.

"We're going to have to keep you under guard until we get into Sky City," Colonel Rivera says. "Sorry, but you're the first outsiders to enter in years, and we've got to be careful."

I think there is a note of glee in his voice when he talks.

"We're not giving up our weapons, if that's what you're asking," Uriah says. He stands next to me, his dark hair catching the breeze. "That's not an option."

I grip the knife on my belt.

I do not waver in my cold, menacing stare. Colonel Rivera must see the danger in my eyes because he says, "You can keep your weapons. But we need to get inside. We've already been out here too long."

I walk near Uriah, and I am surprised to see that half of the guards with Colonel Rivera stay with the plane. Arlene whispers, "They're going to hide it. We like to keep everything invisible from the air, in case Omega does any flyovers."

The other five guards remain with us. They are silent, stoic.

"Are you in charge here, then?" I ask Colonel Rivera.

"I am," he replies.

"No one is necessarily in charge," Arlene corrects. "We take directions from the Pacific Northwest Alliance, from the militias."

"But you have a chain of command, correct?" I ask. "A structure of leadership of some sort?"

"Yes, but..." she trails off. "You'll see."

We walk uphill. It is so silent here. No background noise. No helicopters or fighter jets roaring over our heads. No rumble of Humvees. No clink of metal or conversation.

Nothing but the sound of the wind and the crunch of our boots against the snow and rocks.

"Where are we *going*?" Vera demands.

We reach the top of the slope, round a corner, and there is a large rock shelf here. It overhangs nearly twenty feet, putting the sheer, slippery cliff in the shadow of the shelf. There is a rocky path along the bottom of the cliff. We follow it, and I keep my hand hovering over the gun strapped to my thigh, uneasy in this open environment.

There is a grove of trees to the left of the cliff, and for the first time since arriving, I see signs of security. A tall, nearly invisible metal fence threads through the pines, topped with coils of wicked barbed wire. I see three camouflaged lookout towers hidden in the trees.

"How many snipers do you have guarding the perimeter?" I ask.

"More than meets the eye," Rivera replies.

He does not elaborate, purely because he knows it will irritate me.

Or at least, that's how it comes across.

We come to a large section at the bottom of the rock cliff. Up close, it is obvious that it is a steel door that has been painted the same color as the rock, but from a distance, it's invisible. There is a smooth, black panel on the wall. Colonel Rivera places his palm against it. It scans his hand.

"I haven't seen that kind of technology since before the EMP," Manny comments. "Arlene used to have one of those cell phones that scanned your fingerprint to access the home screen." He shrugs. "Different times."

Arlene tilts her head, verifying the truth of his story.

When the hand scanner is done, it glows green, and the airlock steel entrance opens with a hiss. It slides open, and then I see a long, dark chamber glowing with lights. They flicker orange against the walls.

We step inside, and the airlock shuts quickly behind us.

It seals with an echoing boom, and I get a feeling of claustrophobia.

We are locked in.

*

I watch the burning orange of the sun touch the tips of the pine trees. I sit on the front steps of the cabin called Bear Paw, listening to Sophia shuffle around inside, arranging our things. The meadow to the left of the cabins is covered with soldiers. They are playing a game, tossing Frisbees back and forth, laughing and hollering at the top of their lungs.

I watch them, wishing I felt like joining in.

I feel too tired, though. Plus, my shoulder is still healing from a gunshot wound. It will be sore for a few more days, at least.

"You look depressed," Sophia says in a singsong voice.

I don't look behind me.

"I am," I reply. "I don't deny it. I've got issues."

"What kind of issues?"

"I-got-shot-in-the-shoulder issues," I say, grinning. "It sucks."

"I'll bet." Sophia walks outside and takes a seat beside me on the steps. "I've been meaning to ask you something."

I raise an eyebrow.

"You didn't kill Kamaneva," she says. "You hesitated. Why?"

Kamaneva, the commanding officer of the labor camp.

The woman that very nearly killed me.

"I don't know," I answer. "I guess I just didn't want to stoop to her level."

"But you've killed other Omega soldiers. Why was she different?"

I look into Sophia's eyes, and I see genuine sincerity in her question.

"I felt sorry for her," I say at last. "She was so unhappy, so bitter. I think she would have been happy to be killed. I didn't want to give her that. I wanted to believe that she could change."

"People like that don't change," Sophia mutters.

I shrug.

"Maybe not," I say. "But I keep hoping. Because people who change are going to be the ones who save the

world these days."

Sophia pulls her knees up to her chest.

"I don't know," she answers. "You could be right."

I nod.

"Could be." I move, wincing. My shoulder is extra sore tonight. "Sometimes I feel like there's a lot more going on here than just a war, though. More than just a takeover. It's an annihilation."

Sophia stares at me, then looks back at the meadow.

A yellow Frisbee whizzes over our heads and someone sprints after it.

"That's scary," she says.

"Yeah," I agree. "But it would be scarier if we weren't willing to fight it."

I intend to fight it.

Every day. Until I die.

Or until someone kills me.

*

The orange lights flicker against the dark, steel walls. The wide hallway slopes downward. We are descending into the mountain. As I follow Arlene and Colonel Rivera, I never remove my hand from my knife. I am not afraid, but I am not at ease. I am somewhere between the two.

After a few hundred feet, we come to another steel door. There are two guard posts here, and two guards. They are dressed in standard camouflage uniforms.

They have been expecting us, by the looks of it.

The two guards salute the Colonel and the doors slide open. I figure that someone must be opening them from the other side, because there is nothing out here that would help anyone gain access through these doors – except maybe a cruise missile.

When the doors open, I squint my eyes, nearly blinded by the sudden flow of light. Before us, there is a bunker that must span an entire football field in length. Huge hallways curve in a circle, and above our heads, there is a concave ceiling showering us with white, artificial light.

I'm impressed, but I say nothing.

I look at Elle. She clutches Bravo's harness and catches my eye. She doesn't speak, either, but she nods. Slowly. She is impressed, too.

"Well, this is quite a tin can, Arlene," Manny says.

"It's much more than that," she replies. "The bunker descends twenty levels deeper into the mountain. We have our generators but mainly rely on geothermal energy from the volcanic heart of this mountain to power the base. We have our own food, hydro-farming and meat production. We even have our own weapons manufacturing. Sky City was built to last centuries in the event of a disaster, whether it was a foreign invasion or a nuclear bomb."

Soldiers in Sky City camouflage uniforms scurry to and fro. They don't even notice that we are here, but occasionally someone glances up and looks at Uriah, Manny, Elle and myself.

"This way," Colonel Rivera mutters.

He seems agitated, and I don't blame him.

I don't like him, and he doesn't like me.

But at least we have enough respect for each other to avoid getting into a fist fight – or something stupid like that.

I follow Colonel Rivera down a narrow steel walkway that cuts through the center of the circular bunker. There is an elevator here. The Colonel calls it, the doors open, and we step inside.

"You call it Sky City," Elle says to Arlene. "But there's no sky."

"It's *in* the sky," Arlene replies, giving Elle a loving smile. "We are hidden in the clouds."

"You're hidden in the *rocks*," Manny murmurs.

"How do you get recruited for Sky City?" I ask, curious.

"We come to you," Arlene tells me. "Sky City recruits soldiers secretly. I was recruited when I was young, working with the National Guard. They recruited Manny, also."

I raise an eyebrow.

"You never said anything about Sky City," I say.

"I didn't know it really existed," he replies, shrugging.

"Nobody at our level did, until the EMP," Arlene explains. "And even then, it was only a rumor. We have bases all over the country, but I was never brought in. Not until my home was destroyed by Omega. Then I was relocated here."

The elevator stops at the 12th sub-level. I have to yawn, keeping the pressure from building up in my ears. The doors open, and this level is not as busy as the others. A red *12* is painted on the wall. I step outside. The air is cool, but it smells artificial.

"Smells like plastic," Elle comments.

"We filter the air," Arlene says. "It's a little dry, but it's clean."

There is hardly anyone on this level. I see a sign that says *Officers' Quarters*. We pass it, and continue down the curving hallway to another sign. This one reads: *Meeting Rooms*.

Colonel Rivera pushes one of the doors open and we step into a spacious meeting room. There is a long, dark table and office chairs set up here.

"Well," Colonel Rivera says. "Go on, Commander. Or should I say Senator? Are you still playing both parts?"

I resist the urge to sling back a stinging retort.

Instead, I reply, "What can I say? I enjoy multitasking, Colonel."

I walk to the table. I look at Arlene. "You brought me here to convince your military commander that the West Coast needs reinforcements – strong, capable reinforcements who already understand Omega's fighting tactics. Colonel Rivera already knows this."

I look at Elle.

"I know that you brought your niece with you because she's family and you wanted to keep her safe," I continue. "But you don't need me here. The Colonel knows what's going on down there – if he doesn't send us recruits, that's his fault for condemning us all to death. There's nothing I can say that will change his mind."

I glare at Rivera as I say this, and he returns it.

But he does not argue the point.

Arlene takes a seat in a chair.

"I didn't know that you were formerly acquainted with Colonel Rivera," she admits.

"You should have," I say.

"She's not the all-seeing eye," Manny intervenes. "Sky City doesn't know the connection between every single human being on the face of the planet. For example, they weren't even aware that my own niece was running around in the militias. Nobody told me."

"That was because I kept a low profile," Elle says, almost under her breath.

"Commander Hart," Colonel Rivera booms, "while you're correct in your assumption that I don't want to send my recruits down the mountain – I don't believe we'll do you much good – I am willing to cut you a deal."

I raise an eyebrow.

"You being here is fortuitous, although I'd prefer Chris Young." He balances his cigar between his thumb and middle finger. "I will give you all the recruits you need, if you do me a favor in return."

"I'm not a politician, Rivera," I snap. "Get to the point."

"There's an Omega insurgency camp here in the Sierra Nevada Mountains," he tells me. "They've been training Omega mercenaries and soldiers for years – long before the EMP and the invasion. I'd like you to take them out."

"A *camp*?" I say. "How many soldiers are we talking about?"

"Several hundred," Rivera replies. "Their numbers have increased. They're making no effort to hide their presence since the invasion. I want them dead – all of them. Every last damn one."

There is a glint in his eyes, the fire of a soldier.

And that is the redeeming quality of this stubborn, pig-headed man.

"I want your word," I say.

"You've got it."

"I'm going to need a team."

"I'll give you one."

"And weapons. Vehicles. Everything."

"Commander, you'll get everything you want," Colonel Rivera says, folding his arms across his chest. "We'll give you all the toys, you wipe out the insurgency camp for us, and you can bring back as many troops as you need."

I shake my head.

I should have known there would be a catch.

"Fine," I say. "When do we start?"

Arlene stands up.

"Right away," she smiles.

Her smile is a little too cheerful.

*

The Officers Quarters' are where I am staying. I have a small, private room. In an underground bunker like this, privacy is a luxury. The room is narrow, with a cot, vent, shower and toilet. There are no windows, which reminds me that I am buried alive, hundreds of feet into a rocky mountain.

I try to push the thought away.

I sit down on the edge of the cot – hard as a rock –– and mess with my knife. I remember the day I received it well. I remember how happy Jeff was. So proud.

Someone knocks on my door.

I stand up, opening it. It's Arlene. She isn't smiling now.

"I need to talk to you," she says. And then, in a whisper, she adds, "Inside."

I give her some space and she sweeps into the room. I close and lock the door. "What's going on?" I ask.

She holds a finger to her lips and checks the room – under the mattress, beneath the toilet. Then she says, "Sorry. I had to check for bugs."

"You think someone's spying on us?" I reply.

"I think that what I'm about to tell you is very secret, and I don't want the information falling into the wrong hands." She sits on my bed, sighing. "Cassidy, I trust you. I don't know you very well, but my husband thinks the world of you, and there must be a reason for that."

"Manny's a good man." I cross my arms over my chest and lean against the wall. "What's this all about?"

"The Insurgency Camp," Arlene says. "We've known about it for years. It's existed right under our noses for as long as I can remember, growing and growing. And nobody ever did anything to stop it."

"Why not?" I demand.

"I don't know. That's what bothers me. The decision was never up to me, and it's not really up to Rivera, either." She shrugs. "The thing is, Cassidy, Unite has been controlling Sky City since its inception, and they've been painfully neutral for years. Their focus has always been on survival, not defense."

I close my eyes.

That explains a lot.

Or at least it explains why Sky City has never offered its troops to the militias yet. If their main concern is staying alive, then they might as well be dead to me. They're useless.

"Do you think Rivera is telling the truth?" I ask. "Will he really give me the troops I need if I take out the insurgency camp?"

"I think he will." She pauses. "Rivera is many things, Cassidy, but he is not a liar. He just does what he thinks is best."

"That's a gross understatement."

"Yes. I also wanted to warn you about something."

She looks uncertain, almost afraid. Her voice becomes soft.

"Unite is good," she says. "Their very existence is, in the end, a positive thing. But it's more than meets the eye. And that's all I can say right now. Just...keep that in mind, all right?"

My heartbeat quickens a little.

"You're saying I shouldn't trust Unite?"

"I'm saying you should be careful, that's all." She stands up suddenly, flushing. "I've said too much. You know where my loyalties are, Cassidy. Just remember what I said."

"You didn't say *much*," I remark.

"It's enough. You'll thank me later." She touches my shoulder. "I'm glad you're here. We all appreciate it."

She whisks out of the room, disappearing into the hall. I lock the door behind her and puzzle over her words. Obviously she was trying to warn me, but the total secrecy in which Unite and Sky City has operated since its inception is making it impossible for her to share everything.

I remember the look on her face when she searched the room for bugs.

It was more than fear. Almost...paranoia.

I shake myself.

I open the door and walk into the hall. I follow the curve of the massive, underground rotunda, occasionally passing other officers. They give me a once-over and keep walking. I guess I'm the new meat around here – I don't mind. I might be new to these people, but *I'm* not new to this situation.

I've probably got a better grasp than they do.

I'm the one who's actually been out there.

These people have been hiding in a hole in the ground.

"Cassidy?"

I turn around. Elle jogs up to me. Bravo is not with her.

"Where's Bravo?" I ask.

"He's resting in our room." She tucks a piece of short, black hair behind her ear. "So when are we going to do it?"

"Do what?"

I keep walking, and she keeps pace.

"Take out the Omega insurgency training camp."

"As soon as Rivera gives me a team and weapons," I tell her.

"I want to come."

I smile.

"That's very nice of you, but I can't allow that."

"Why not? I'm a good soldier. I don't follow you around with a bomb dog all day long for nothing, you know." She shakes her head. "I can help you."

"I know you can." I stop, put one hand on each of her shoulders, and look into her blue eyes. "But it's too dangerous. And I'm sure Manny and Arlene would tell you the same thing."

She rolls her eyes.

We keep walking until we reach the Chow Hall. It's a large room with rows and rows of plastic tables, similar to many other dining halls I've seen before. This one is crowded with people. It is a wall of noise, a rush of jumbled dialogue and laughter. And then there is the smell: meat and garlic.

"Wow, I'm hungry," I say. "How about you?"

"Yes, ma'am."

We walk into the Chow Hall, grab a plate, and get in line.

"I just think that you should let me come," Elle says again.

"Elle, have you ever had any combat experience besides using Bravo?" I ask. "Do you know what it's like to be on the front lines of a fight? It's scary."

"I know," she insists. "You have no idea what I've had to do to survive."

I hold out my plate for a spoonful of roast beef.

"Have you ever killed a man?" I ask.

She closes her mouth. We go through the line, find a seat, and pick up our forks. She looks at me and says at last, "Yes."

"Who?"

She sighs.

"The first time I killed someone, it was in self defense," she replies. "In Los Angeles. He was a member of a gang called the Klan, a vigilante anarchist group. He was going to kill me. I shot him. After that, I killed again." She looks straight at me. "I've lost count, Commander."

I take a deep breath, jarred by the realization that this young girl has so much blood on her hands. It's a stark reminder of what the world has become.

"That scar on your cheek," I say. "Where'd you get it?"

"Fell down a hill," she grins. "Cut it open."

"Ouch."

"Could have been worse, believe me."

I take a few more bites, savoring the rich, hearty flavor.

"What happened to your family?" I ask at last.

She stares at the floor.

"Don't know," she replies. "My dad…he used to be in retail. He had an organic grocery store in Los Angeles. Then he became a celebrity lawyer. Don't know how he made that transition, but he did. My mom was an actress."

"Anyone famous?" I smile.

"No. Never got the chance." She shrugs. "My brother was a great violinist, but he got into drugs and he was in jail when the EMP went down. They're all dead, probably."

"I'm sorry, Elle," I tell her. And I mean it.

"I've got Aunt and Uncle."

"Arlene and Manny are good people. You're lucky." She nods.

"How did you end up joining the militias?" I ask. "How'd you get separated from your folks?"

"It's a long story," she says.

"I've got time."

"Well..."

She fixes her blue eyes on the far side of the room, suddenly tensing up. I follow her gaze. There is a commotion at the entrance of the Chow Hall. Soldiers are milling around in a small group, and in the middle of the crowd, I see Uriah pushing his way through.

I stand up, alarmed.

He runs toward us.

"Cassidy," he says. "Come quick."

"What's happening?"

He catches his breath. I notice that he is sweating, and that there is a spray of blood on his right cheek. "Come on," he urges.

I follow him, pushing through the crowd.

"Uriah!" I say. "What's going on?"

He doesn't reply. We run through the hall. Everyone has stopped just outside of the Officers' Quarters. There are red lights flashing near the ceiling, and somewhere in the distance, a siren screams through the upper chambers of the bunker.

What I see next stops me.

Manny is kneeling on the floor. Arlene is in his arms, limp. Tears stream down his face. Elle rushes forward, sinking to the floor, touching Arlene's throat. She covers her mouth, crying out. Arlene's face is pale and her body is still.

I feel sick. I take a step backward.

Just a few feet away from Arlene, a dead body is on the floor. His arm is twisted at an unnatural angle, and I can tell that it has been broken. His head is tilted sideways, too. His eyes are wide open and glassy.

His neck has been snapped.

I gasp.

Lieutenant Alan White.

Chapter Seven

Killing has become too easy for me.

I lie prone in the grass. We have just left Sector 20, on our second mission into the surrounding urban areas in the Central Valley. Our job is to remove Omega threats. I have been given a new uniform by the National Guard. I am not used to working with the military, but I am sure that I will adjust.

I see an Omega patrol in the distance, past the grass, in a parking lot.

It is a small one. Three trucks and a Humvee parked next to an old propane tank. The troops are milling around in their dark uniforms, talking and laughing. They look relaxed. Too relaxed. They should know that this area is crawling with militia activity – they should not be this careless.

Behind me, there is an earsplitting crack. I try to turn my head, but I'm flattened against the ground. A flash of light and a wave of heat hits my body.

What was that?

After the shockwave rolls over me, I force myself up and turn around. Two hundred yards off, in a ditch, there is a ring of fire. A pillar of thick, dark smoke rises into the air.

I don't dare move. I haven't received any orders on my radio.

I don't want to be the one to give our snipers' positions away.

I tilt my head and look through the scope of my rifle again. The Omega troops that I have been watching are inside their vehicles, now, speeding away. I curse under my breath. My radio crackles, but I cannot hear what the command is. My ears are still ringing from the explosion in the ditch.

I make an executive decision.

I squeeze the trigger of my rifle and put an armor-piercing bullet through the center of the propane tank. The metal container detonates in a brilliant ball of orange flames and black smoke. The heat from the explosion burns my skin. I bury my face in the crook of my elbow to protect my eyes from injury as shrapnel spins through the air.

I look up at last. The small patrol vehicles have been scattered across the pavement. The Humvee is on fire and the trucks are sideways. I watch carefully, looking for any signs of movement.

Sweat rolls down my forehead, dripping into my eyes.

I wipe it away and stare through my optics. After several long minutes, there is a flicker. A small flash. The car door on one of the overturned trucks is kicked open and an Omega trooper crawls out. His face and chest are bloody. The right side of his cheek is burned. He pulls himself forward on his hands, dragging his body across the asphalt.

My sights are clearly set on the center of his forehead.

My finger hovers over the trigger.

Something stops me. In my mind, I see an innocent, peaceful girl covering her eyes during a violent movie. The girl is me. I shake myself and blink the memory away.

I take the shot. The trooper's head jerks backward and his body hits the ground at a weird angle, halfway twisted toward the sky. Dead. I rest my shoulder against my rifle and stand. I turn away from the wreckage of the patrol and trot to the ditch, where the initial explosion came from earlier.

I peer over the edge. Three of our men are dead, literally blown to pieces. Blood and gore drip down the side of the ditch closest to me. I take a step backward and fight the urge to vomit.

"Landmines."

Alexander Ramos kneels on the other side of the ditch. He rests his powerful forearm on his knee. "Poor bastards," he mutters.

My radio crackles.

"Yankee One, this is Alpha One."

"Copy, Alpha One," I reply. "Go ahead."

"Nice shot. You made the surprise party a success."

Although hearing Chris's voice makes me smile, a deep, overwhelming sense of sadness overcomes me. I look at the dead men in the ditch – our men. Human beings, torn apart and scattered in the dirt.

I turn away.

"Yankee One, you still with me?" Chris says over the radio.

"Yeah," I whisper. "I think so."

*

The casualty care center in Sky City is a wide, spacious floor with gurneys and rollaway room dividers. There are not many patients here. Apparently Sky City is a healthy place.

Arlene is lying on her back in a gurney, a tube down her throat, pumping oxygen into her chest. Her skin is horribly white, tinged with purple. Manny sits on a chair near her, holding her hand, staring at her still, lifeless form.

Elle stands at the foot of the bed, silent.

"There was a struggle," Vera tells me. "She and Alan fought for a few seconds – he tried to choke her. He almost succeeded."

We are at the end of the hall. It's all white light and antiseptic in here as medical aides scurry around, trying to quell the surge of panic inside the bunker.

Lieutenant Alan White's dead body is on a gurney near the door. The deep purple bruises around his neck tell me that he was choked to death.

"I saw it happen," Vera goes on, flicking her ponytail behind her shoulder. "Arlene was walking around the corner, toward her room in the Officers' Quarters. He was just walking, Cassidy. *Walking*. And then he was going for her head, probably trying to snap her neck."

I inhale.

"Who killed Alan?" I ask.

"I did."

I raise an eyebrow.

"You choked him out like that?" I say.

"Uriah helped." She shrugs. "I did what I had to do."

I nod. "I'm glad you did."

I look at Alan. "Why would he do this?"

"He's another Omega hack. He has to be."

"You don't think it's just a case of one man snapping under the pressure of the apocalypse?"

Vera gives me a look.

We both know that's not true.

I walk over to Alan and pull the sheet away from his chest. He's dressed in standard military garb. I turn away from his dead body.

I have never seen Manny look so forlorn before. He holds her hand tightly, staring at her pale face.

It's a miracle that she's still alive.

"I'm sorry you have to go through this," I whisper, placing my hand on Manny's shoulder.

He says nothing. Elle stands behind him with her dog, silent. Her face looks like it's made of stone. She betrays nothing.

"I want to know why the hell Alan White would try to kill Arlene in the middle of a secure facility," Uriah mutters. "How did he think he would get away with that?"

No one answers. Because nobody knows.

At that moment, Colonel Rivera enters the medical chamber. He is not smoking a cigar. In fact, he looks drawn – worried. He stops at the foot of Arlene's bed. "I'm sorry this happened," he says after a long silence.

I meet his gaze. While I do not like Rivera, I see sincerity in his eyes.

He seems genuinely sorry to see Arlene in this state.

"Why would Lieutenant White do this?" Vera says.

"Because he's an Omega spy," Uriah replies. "Just like Sophia was."

I wince, hearing Sophia's name.

Her death and betrayal is still a fresh wound.

"Sophia *Rodriguez*?" Rivera asks.

I nod to confirm.

He shakes his head.

"I'm...sorry to hear that, too," he says.

I cross my arms over my chest, wondering why he's being so apologetic. And then I realize that Arlene was probably a good friend of his, and seeing her struggling for her life on a hospital bed is not just emotional for us – but for him, too. Proving that, despite all evidence to the contrary, Colonel Rivera might have a heart after all.

"What's our next move, Commander?" Uriah asks.

I tear my eyes away from Arlene.

What *is* our next move?

"Excuse us." A young Sky City officer walks into the room. He is followed by a group of soldiers – I quickly count fifteen. He is tall, handsome. Very young. His hair is shaved to the scalp, his skin is pale, his eyes are blue. "Sorry for the inconvenience," he continues. He flicks his finger, and every gun on every guard is pointed straight at all of us. "But we're going to have to ask you to come with us."

I place my palm on the handgun holstered on my belt.

"What?" I say, shocked. "By whose orders?"

He doesn't reply.

"Lower your weapons," he says instead. "And no one will get hurt."

A sick feeling seeps into the pit of my stomach as I watch the faces in the room – all sixteen of them, cold, detached and unflinching. I look at the young officer. "Who are you?" I ask.

"Lieutenant Connor," he replies. "Now, Commander." He points to the ground. "All weapons on the ground."

"No," Vera spits. "What is this all about?"

"No," Colonel Rivera says, storming in front of me. "Stand down. Lieutenant Alan White is already dead – nobody here is under suspicion of having anything to do with the incident involving Arlene Costas." He narrows his eyes. "I'll say it one more time: stand down."

Connor holds his handgun level with Colonel Rivera's forehead.

"No, Colonel," he says coldly. Emotionless. "*You* stand down."

Several long, tense seconds tick by. Colonel Rivera glares at the young Connor. He moves his hand toward his gun holster, then brings it back up again, punching Connor right in the jaw. The boy flies backward, blood bubbling out of the side of his mouth. There is a gunshot, and Colonel Rivera jerks backward, hitting the foot of Arlene's hospital bed.

I leap into action, snapping my handgun out of my holster. Vera drops to a crouch, whipping out her gun, but three Sky City guards collide with her, bringing her down to the floor. She is a vicious fighter, taking off pieces of their hair and tearing bloody gashes into their skin.

I fire two shots, taking down two of the officers. But there are more coming. Manny swings up behind him, bringing a revolver out from beneath his leather duster. He fires off three shots. One of them ricochets off the wall. I duck. Uriah smashes his fist into the side of a guard's face. Somewhere in the distance, an alarm sounds. Red lights flash in the medical chamber.

There is yelling and screaming. Out of the corner of my eye, I see Bravo shoot away from Elle and sink his fangs into a trooper's arm. He screams, scrambling for his gun. I shoot him before he can reach his holster.

Elle pulls her own handgun from her holster, a 1911 Smith and Wesson. She doesn't hesitate before she squeezes the trigger, nailing one guard in the chest. Uriah spins around me and blocks my right side from an oncoming guard.

My heart is pounding in my ears, my blood is rushing through my veins. I have a heightened sense of hearing and an improved reaction time. One trooper grabs my shoulders and slams me against the wall. I feel the air go out of my lungs as his fingers dig into my throat. I struggle for air, feeling my face go red. Black spots dance around the edges of my vision.

I drop my gun and bring my hands up to his face, pushing my thumbs into the corners of his eyes. I dig deeper and deeper until blood gushes out, streaming down his cheeks. He screams and backs away, holding his hands against his face. I cough, trying to catch my breath, sliding to the floor, grabbing my gun. I slam the weapon against the back of his head, knocking him, unconscious, to the floor.

One, two, five, seven...there are still nine guards left, and more are pouring into the room. I share a split second glance with Uriah, and then Manny. Uriah shakes his head.

We are outnumbered, trapped.

Countless troops come into the room, pushing us against the wall. Shooting and cutting through as many as we can, they finally pin us into the corner, away from Arlene's still form on the bed.

I throw my weapons on the ground, as does the rest of my team – all except Manny. Three guards wrestle him to the floor, pinning his arms behind him. They smack his face onto the ground. Blood streams from the sides of his mouth. I fight, claw, kick, and twist away from the troops, but it's no use. A solid wall of nearly thirty guards fence us in.

The officer named Connor works his way to the front. He wipes the blood from his mouth, spits on Colonel Rivera, and turns to me.

"You belong to us, now," Connor says.

Elle struggles against her captors as two troops grab Bravo, one wrestling his head, pressing it against the floor, the other slamming the dog's body flat, slipping a muzzle over his snarling fangs.

"Don't touch my dog!" Elle screams.

Connor smacks Elle across the face. She curses him – loudly – and he smiles.

"Take them all below," he replies.

"What's going on?" Colonel Rivera demands. "This bull does *not* fly with me, Lieutenant. You're going to—"

"Shut up, Colonel," Connor says, a demure smile on his face. "You're not in charge here. You never *were*. The only thing keeping you alive is what's inside your head – which, although not much, may be valuable to us."

A terrifying chill crawls up my spine.

Us.

We are dragged out of the medical chamber.

Manny shouts all the way, fighting and struggling against

the troops. I do, too, for a while, until I realize that my attempts are futile.

We are inside a secure base, locked in a steel box, hundreds of feet underground.

There *is* no escape.

We're taken to an elevator, shoved inside, gun muzzles digging into the back of our necks, and we arrive at the lowest level. We walk through the curved hallway, stopping at a steel door. Connor opens it with an access card and we are pushed through. I swallow a lump in my throat.

This is the cellblock. Basic iron bars span the length of the room. About ten cells in all. Each one has a toilet and a cot – nothing more. The lights are dim down here, a dull orange glow. I am shoved into the first cell. Elle goes into the next. Everyone gets their own cell – even Bravo.

"Dammit, Connor," Rivera growls. "What's this all about?"

Connor pauses at the door. A smile curls at the corner of his mouth, and for a moment, I get a flash of Harry Lydell's face in him.

"All hail to the New Order," Connor says.

And that tells us everything we need to know.

Sky City is not safe.

Sky City is under Omega control.

Chapter Eight

"How is this even *possible*!?" Vera screeches. She paces her cell like a nervous animal. "How could Unite – how could Sky City – be infiltrated by Omega? Arlene swore it was safe!"

"Apparently she was wrong." Uriah sits on the floor of his cell, staring at the wall, strangely calm. "Apparently we all were."

The cellblock is cold and stale, dark and shadowy.

"Arlene was trying to warn me about Unite earlier today," I say. "Before Alan White got to her. She must have known that she was being watched. And then they tried to kill her."

"So why would they treat her in the hospital if they wanted her dead?" Elle demands. She's standing at the bars of her cell, a pensive expression on her face. "Why not just kill *all* of us now?"

"We wouldn't be alive if we didn't have something that they want," I reply. "And, knowing Omega, what they want is information. Troop movements, the location of militia leaders. Anything that they could use to bring us down. And then they'll kill us."

Vera slams her fist against the wall.

"I can't believe this. I can't believe we walked straight into an Omega hive." She shakes her head. "We're dead. It's over."

"Wow, always so optimistic," I remark. "Thanks for that."

"I'm stating facts, Cassidy." She shrugs. "Nobody's coming to rescue us. Nobody even knows this place exists – and who knows if Chris or anybody in Monterey even knows the coordinates of our location." She leans against the wall. "Yeah. We're screwed."

Manny is oddly quiet.

I suppose his thoughts are with his comatose wife in the medical chambers.

Have they killed her? Is she still alive?

"Our chances of survival," Colonel Rivera says suddenly, "are slim to none."

I roll my eyes.

"Thanks for the commentary, sunshine," I mutter.

I shake myself and walk back and forth in the cell. I am afraid – *very* afraid. There is no realistic way to survive a situation like this. Trapped inside an Omega base, surrounded by enemies.

What would Chris have me do? I ask myself. *How would he get out of here?*

I struggle to grasp onto the thread of any idea that might help us, but I come up short. All we can do is wait and see what they want with us.

And hope we don't die by tonight.

"Someone's coming," Elle says suddenly.

Bravo's ears flatten against his head. He growls softly.

The doorway at the end of the hall opens.

The young officer named Connor walks in, clad in his Sky City combat fatigues, a snide smile on his lips. "Commander Hart," he says simply.

There are four guards with him. They open my cell door, and I am escorted into the hallway. Uriah stands at the bars of his cell.

"Hey, where you taking her?" he demands.

No answer.

"Hey!" Uriah raises his voice, and I can see the anger burning in his coal colored eyes. "If you do anything to hurt her—"

Connor stops in front of Uriah.

He says, "There's nothing you can do to stop me."

They whisk me into the hall. My friends disappear behind me as the door slams shut, and I am brought through the halls, into another room behind the cellblock. We walk through a steel door, into a clean, plain chamber with dim lighting. There is one guard in each corner of the room, in addition to the four guards escorting me.

There is a low, square tub in the center of the room. It is sloped down in the back, filled with water. A rush of fear hits me, and I find myself struggling to breathe.

"Commander Hart," Connor says. He motions to his guards, and they step away from me, leaving me standing free in the center of the room, facing Connor. The lock on the door clicks shut, and I am trapped with eight guards and one homicidal maniac.

Fun times.

"This is how we're going to conduct this interrogation," he continues. "You're going to tell me what I want to know, and I'll let you go back to your cell. Or, you can resist, and you will tell me what I want to know eventually. Either way, the endgame is the same. I get what I want, and you get nothing." He folds his hands together. "Understand?"

I raise an eyebrow.

I am terrified, but I do not show it.

"How long has Sky City been under Omega control?" I ask.

He laughs aloud, rolls his eyes and steps close to me.

"Since the beginning," he says in a low voice. "You were a fool to come here, Commander. And after I've squeezed every bit of information out of you and your companions, your deaths will be reason for Omega followers to rejoice."

For the first time since I have met Connor, I hear the hint of an accent in his voice – he sounds German. I don't answer him. I can't think of anything to say – anything *appropriate*, anyway. I don't want to poke a stick. Not now. I have no leverage.

"So, Commander," Connor continues. "Are you going to help me out?"

"I have no intention of helping anyone," I reply, "except for my men."

"I want to know who knows that you're here in Sky City," he goes on, ignoring me. "I want to know how long it will be until someone comes looking for you. I want to know how many troops you have left in Monterey. I want to know the name and location of every militia commander from here to Washington State." He tilts his head. "Start talking, Commander."

I purse my lips.

"I can't help you," I say quietly.

"I see." He lifts a finger. "Fine. We'll do it my way, then."

Two of the guards take my wrists and tie them together with a plastic zip-tie. It cuts into my wrists and draws blood. I wince. They drag me to the square tub and lean my head back. My head sinks into the water as two guards hold down my feet and two more hold my shoulders. Connor stands at over my head, leering at me with grim satisfaction. A fifth guard takes a cloth, soaks it in water, and holds it over my face. I can't see anything, I can't hear anything. They pour water over the cloth, and I can feel it running down my nose and throat. I can't breathe. I choke and sputter, jerking forward, panicking. I know I'm not really drowning – I know that this is just a simulation, but it feels real.

Water bubbles out of my mouth. Just when I think I'm going to get a deep breath, more water floods down my throat, burns my nostrils. I choke again, and I frantically struggle against the arms holding me down.

They dunk my head completely under the water. I want to scream, but I can't. My lungs burn. My mind races. My heart is thumping loudly in my ears. They pull my head out of the water, rip the towel off my face, and I vomit all over myself. I barely catch a breath before Connor grabs my chin and holds it, his fingernails digging into my skin, his thumb on my lip.

"Would you consider talking now, Commander?" he asks.

I bite his thumb, crunching his bone between my teeth. He screams, shrieking profanities, shoving my head back into the water. The towel comes back, the water rushes into my mouth and my nose.

I'm drowning again.

And it doesn't stop for a very long time.

*

When I wake up, I'm back in the cellblock. My head is squished up against the bars, and someone has their hand in my hair. I jump up, gasping for breath.

"Cassidy, it's me!"

Elle grasps the cell bars. She holds out her hand.

"It's just me," she says again, softer.

I look down at my shirt. I am disgusting. My jacket is still wet, soaked with water and vomit. I taste blood in my mouth. I feel exhausted, as if someone dropped a weight on my head.

"Cassidy, I'm so sorry," Elle whispers.

I lick my lips, swallow.

"It's all good," I say, but my voice is raspy.

Uriah gets to his feet across the hall, looking at me. His eyes are sad.

"Are you okay?" he asks.

I shrug.

I'm not really sure how to answer that question.

I look into Manny's cell. He is sitting on the floor, his back to the room, his head bent over. He is asleep. Poor guy – it must be horrible, knowing your wife is just out of your reach.

"Did you give them any information?" Vera asks harshly.

I peer at her silhouette in the dark room. She leans forward.

"No," I reply. "Why would I?"

"I'm just asking." She frowns. "I'm sorry."

I shrug again.

I draw my knees up to my chest. I feel weak all over. My throat burns like fire, both from the torture and from screaming too much. At least I didn't tell Connor anything. I still have some of my dignity, I guess.

Chris would be proud.

"What did they want to know?" Vera asks.

"Vera, leave her—" Uriah begins, but Vera cuts him off.

"We need to *know*," she says. "Like Cassidy said. We wouldn't be alive if we didn't have something they wanted."

"They want to know where every militia commander is on the west coast," I say. "Honestly, I don't really know. I know where some of them are. But militias like us? We stay hidden. They wanted to know everything I knew, basically." I stop talking, because my throat hurts too much. "No more questions right now," I tell them.

I close my eyes.

I am too tired to think. Too tired to move.

The hallway door slams open. I wince and draw back, terrified.

I don't know if I can survive more interrogation.

This time, however, it isn't me that they come for. I don't recognize Connor among the guards. But I *do* recognize the person that they are dragging along the floor. They open a cell next to Manny and throw a woman inside.

Arlene.

"Arlene!" Manny exclaims. He presses himself against the bars and reaches through, struggling to stretch out his fingers and touch her limp form. "Arlene! Honey, wake up!"

The guards make a few snide comments and leave the cellblock.

"Is she alive?" Elle asks, standing on tiptoes, straining to see her aunt.

"I don't know," Manny replies grimly.

Arlene lay on her side, her face turned away from me. She is dressed in simple green pants, boots and a white shirt. But she never moves. Manny sits there, his arms through the bars, talking softly to himself – or to Arlene – and willing her to wake up.

I lay my head against the cold floor.

And I am swallowed up by the darkness.

*

I wake up again, and when I do, the first thing I notice is that I'm incredibly hungry. My stomach growls. As I sit up, the cell spins around me, and I'm struck with a sense of clarity: *I am in prison. I have been tortured. I am going to die.*

Wow. I really don't see how this situation could get any worse.

I am afraid, but I am also calm. As a soldier, I live with the threat of death every day. It's nothing new. But sitting in a cell, waiting for someone to kill you is somehow worse than being on the front lines of a fight.

It's like waiting for a bomb to detonate in your hands.

"She's awake," I hear Uriah say.

He's kneeling at his cell. He looks worn. There is a fresh bruise on his cheek – and I know immediately that Uriah has been interrogated, too. I shake my head.

All of this pain...and for what?

We came to Sky City to recruit troops for the militia.

What a useless mission. We'll die here, in a hole in the ground, and no one will ever know what happened to us. I curl my fingers into fists, furious.

I wish there were some way to make Omega pay.

Some way to turn the tables, to take them down.

I try to talk, but my voice is still nothing but a soft whisper. My throat burns like fire, and every time I swallow, I get a horrible flashback of the interrogation – Connor's smug, leering face and endless hands holding my head underwater, drowning me.

I shudder.

"That's a girl," Manny says.

At first I think that he is talking to me, but when I turn around, he's kneeling, speaking to Arlene through the cell bars. Arlene is sitting up, leaning against the bars, holding Manny's hand. Her face is pale, powdery white. Her wavy gray hair, usually in a messy coif on top of her head, is hanging in strands to her shoulders. She looks infinitely older – infinitely more tired.

There is a bandage around her neck. She touches it with her fingers and then touches her lips, slowly shaking her head.

"I understand, my girl," Manny says, using his fondest term of endearment. "I know. I'm sorry."

Arlene shakes her head again.

She locks gazes with me, and her eyes widen.

Cassidy, she mouths.

"Arlene," I whisper.

She nods.

She looks around the cellblock. Rivera is hunched in a tight ball on his cot. Elle is brushing Bravo's coat with her fingers through the bars. Vera is pacing again, and Uriah is sitting. Everyone looks exhausted. Spent.

Arlene taps on the bars with her fingers.

I lean forward.

She points to herself, then to all of us. Her tired, watery eyes crinkle with amusement as everyone stops to watch her, like a sad game of charades.

"You want us to do something," Elle says.

She smiles, bobbing her head.

She points to herself again, then touches her temple, then draws a circle with a tree in the center of it in the air.

"You know something about Sky City," Vera states. "What?"

Arlene pauses for a moment, weary, then leans forward. She drags her finger along the accumulation of dirt and dust on the floor. In big, bold letters she writes:

ESCAPE

"You know a way out," I say.

"Oh, my god," Vera sighs. "Finally."

Arlene looks for another patch of dust on the floor. She draws a circle, carefully illustrating what seems to be the thirteenth level of Sky City. She draws the cellblocks, the communications center, and the arsenal. She pauses, looking up to make sure that we're all following her.

She draws an X on the corner of the map, near the arsenal.

"Is that a way out?" Vera asks.

Arlene raises her hands, yes.

"What is it?" Elle says.

Arlene sighs. It must be frustrating, being unable to communicate what she's thinking. She looks at Manny, then draws a long pathway from the corner of the X, stopping suddenly. She then draws a tree.

"It's a passageway," Manny says. "Well, how about that. Sky City's got more secrets than my mother-in-law when Arlene and I got married."

Arlene gives him a sharp look.

"Sorry, love," he grins. "But we all know the woman had issues."

Arlene looks at all of us.

It's an escape, she mouths. *I can get us out.*

She reaches into her pocket, holding up her access card.

"They didn't take it away from you?" Vera gasps.

"Didn't think of it, most likely," Manny replies. "With all of the commotion we stirred up in the medical chamber, they probably never thought to check Arlene for weapons or valuables since she was already in the hospital."

I fold my hands together under my chin.

"So. There's a back door out of Sky City," I say. My voice is soft and my throat still hurts, but I make an effort to project my words so that everyone can hear. "All we've got to do is get from point A to point B."

"Impossible," Vera replies. "We're locked up in a cell, in case you hadn't noticed."

"I *noticed*," I reply. "There's a way. We just have to think this thing out."

"Cassidy," Uriah says. "When they interrogated me, Connor threatened to kill all of us – soon. We're not giving them any valuable information. They have no reason to keep us alive."

"So we need to hurry." Colonel Rivera suddenly chimes into the conversation. "You're all supposedly military geniuses – come up with a plan."

I smile.

"Challenge accepted," I say.

Chapter Nine

I stand up and lean against the cell bars. I watch Uriah. He is sitting in the corner of his cell, quiet. I do not doubt that the torturous interrogation that he endured from Connor was just as traumatizing as mine – if not worse.

I run a hand through my dirty, unwashed hair.

How long have we been prisoners here?

Two days? Four?

I don't know. I've lost track of time. The absence of daylight in the bunker is confusing. There is no separation between night and day. My internal clock is screwed up.

"Are you ready?" Elle whispers.

She is kneeling on the floor, one arm leaning against her knee. She looks old and wise at that moment, and I find myself smiling.

"Yeah," I say. "You?"

She nods.

I give her two thumbs up.

I am dizzy and lightheaded. I haven't eaten in at least two days – possibly longer, if my internal clock is as messed up as I think it is. The food rations that we've been given in the cellblock have been barely enough to keep a flea alive – plus, I've been unconscious during mealtimes.

My stomach growls. Loudly.

Elle hides a grin behind her hand.

"Somebody get this girl a hamburger," Manny grins. His weathered, wrinkled face looks calm and collected. Despite the situation, he is happy just being near his wife – and knowing that she is alive. "I'm ready to go home. How about you, my girl?"

I smile.

"More than ever," I reply.

Boom, boom, boom.

Footsteps outside in the bunker hallway shake me out of our conversation. I tense. Uriah suddenly sits up straight and rolls to his feet, coming to the corner of his cell. Manny does the same, so that they are standing near each other.

The door opens with a bang, shedding white light into the dim cellblock. Two guards walk inside, each of them with miniscule food rations in their hands.

"Breakfast time," the first one says, tossing something into my cell. I don't move to pick it up. It looks like a plastic bag of beef jerky.

"Come on, red," he sneers at me. "Eat up."

As tempting as it is to eat, I pick it up and toss it through the bars, across the hall, and straight into Uriah's cell.

A boisterous, boyish grin spreads across his face.

"Thanks!" he yells.

One of the guards curses me and reaches through the bars, making a lunge for me. I grab his outstretched arm and snap it sideways against the metal. He screams. I can see the outline of white bone protruding through his flesh. The guard with him charges toward my cell, but I am just out of his reach, keeping a firm grip on the first guard's arm. He continues to scream, overwhelmed with agonizing pain.

His companion – a guard with short black hair – swipes an access card through a computerized panel on my cell. The door pops open and he hurries inside to stop me. I let go of the guard's arm, take a step back, and duck just out of his reach, rolling into the hallway. He spins around, confused. And then he realizes that I am no longer in my cell – *he* is.

I am so tired – starved, dehydrated and beaten from torture – but I am filled with adrenaline. And that is what gives me the strength to kick him in the chin. His head slams against the cell bars. I grab the collar of his shirt and slam him against the bars two more times, shoving him across the hall. Uriah and Manny grab his head and shoulders.

Uriah twists his neck. There is a sickening crack, and all is silent, except for the quiet whimpers of the guard with the broken arm. I lean down, grab the dead guard's access card, and swipe open the cell locks for Uriah, Manny, Arlene, Colonel Rivera, Bravo and Elle.

Uriah kneels down and relieves the dead guard of his gun and magazines. He stands up and takes the conscious guard, slams the butt of the rifle against his head, and he goes limp – out like a light. I take his weapons and belt, then sling the rifle over my shoulder.

Elle gathers up the food rations that have been dropped onto the ground and stuffs them into her jacket. Smart girl. Heart pounding against my ribcage, I motion toward the door.

We have *maybe* sixty seconds to make it down the hall before someone notices what's happened in the cellblock. Guards regularly patrol this level, and I don't want to blow our only chance to escape.

Manny slips his arm around Arlene's waist. She looks pale and weak – I hope she can keep up with us. But I figure Manny will take care of that.

We move to the end of the hall, falling into team formation. It is so natural, we don't even have to think about it. Uriah heads up the front, I follow, then Manny, Arlene, Colonel Rivera, Elle and Bravo, and then Vera brings up the rear.

Uriah slips into the hallway. Although the artificial white light of the bunker is dim compared to natural light, it seems to sear my eyes after being trapped in a shadowy cell for days.

My eyes water as we run down the hall, keeping close to the wall. There is no one in sight…until we round the corner. We follow the curve of the wall, looking at Arlene. She is breathing hard, pointing to the right.

There are only so many places you can go in a place that curves in a circle, so we keep moving forward. I keep the rifle that I took from the guard tucked into my shoulder.

"Whoa, heads up!" Uriah shouts.

I duck. A gunshot flies over my head. Three guards are coming up behind us. I whirl around and slide into a kneeling position, popping off three shots.

Hit, hit, hit.

I may be tired, but my aim is still as good as ever.

Three dead guards hit the ground, blood soaking through their fatigues, staining the floor. I get to my feet, never looking back. Bravo growls.

We run.

We reach the corner – the place that Arlene marked with an X on her map in the cellblock. The arsenal is on the left – a huge steel door.

"We should take weapons!" Vera yells.

"No time!" I say.

A siren screams in the distance. The cellblock is flashing with red lights.

"We're dead if we don't hurry up!" Elle warns.

The corner between the arsenal and cellblock is a simple door. It's unmarked, steel. Nothing special. Arlene throws her card to me. I catch it neatly in the palm of my hand and slide it through the panel near the door.

I pray to God under my breath, willing the computer system to accept it.

The panel blinks green.

I breathe out.

A gunshot echoes through the halls. It ricochets off the steel walls, making my head ring. Uriah fires off two shots. Guards are pouring out of the elevator, coming toward us from both sides of the rotunda.

The door opens.

"Go, move it!!" I yell.

My throat is tight, burning. I keep shouting despite the pain.

Manny goes first with Arlene, then Elle, Bravo and Vera.

"Go on!" I tell Colonel Rivera.

"We won't make it – there's too many, Hart!" he replies.

"JUST GO!" I command.

He hesitates, but only for a moment. He swallows his defiance and runs through the door. I go next, and Uriah follows last. He shuts the door and it seals with a click. We find ourselves in a small hallway.

"What the hell is *this*?" Vera screams, panicked. "There are no doors! It's a box!"

Arlene rushes to the end of the hall. It looks like a garage door. She makes a wind up motion with her fingers.

"It's an emergency hatch," Manny says.

There's one more access panel. Arlene slides her card through, and it blinks green once more. The guards outside hit the door with their weapons. Gunshots echo against the walls.

It's only a matter of seconds before they unlock the door.

The metal panel on the wall rolls up. Behind that, there are two steel doors. They slide open. It's an elevator. I don't even have the time to be impressed. I just run inside with the rest of my team. Arlene slams her fist against a single button, glowing red, on the wall. The doors begin to slide shut just as the guards break through the door at the end of the hall. They sprint toward us. It is a solid barrage of gunfire and yelling.

The steel doors shut.

The elevator drops.

"Oh, my god," Vera says. "Where is this thing taking us?"

Arlene points down.

Vera rolls her eyes.

I am sweating, buzzing. I look at Uriah. He touches my hand – briefly – and then the elevator stops. I tense, look at Arlene, and she nods.

The doors open slowly.

I brace myself for an attack, but there is nothing. Only darkness.

Uriah is the first one to step out of the elevator. As he crosses the threshold, motion sensors catch his movement, and lights flicker on. We are in some kind of underground passage. About a hundred yards down the hall, there's another steel door.

"We can't let the elevator go back up there," Elle says.

"We'll destroy it," Colonel Rivera replies.

I exit the elevator. It's cold down here. Silent.

It's unsettling, like being buried alive.

I look down at the belt that I took from the guard in the cellblock. There's a couple of grenades there. Manny wiggles his eyebrows.

"You send that grenade up there, you'd better make sure the elevator leaves fast," Uriah warns.

I don't disagree.

I look at Arlene.

"It *will* go back up, right?" I ask.

She bobs her head, yes.

I pop a grenade off the belt and hold it in my hand. I look at the elevator.

"Okay," I say. "Here we go!"

When everyone has cleared the elevator, the doors begin to slide shut. I pull the ring on the grenade and toss it inside. We run to the end of the hall, toward the last set of steel doors in the hallway. The elevator leaves our level. I hear a deafening boom as the grenade detonates in the shaft. Something explodes – I hear a cable snap, slamming against the inside of the wall.

"Open it, Arlene!" Manny says.

The passageway rumbles. Arlene opens the last access hatch. The airlock in the wall opens with a hiss.

Everyone rushes through it. I am the last one through, pulling the airlock shut behind me.

We are locked in total darkness.

The silence of the tunnel is deafening – if that's even possible.

"Anyone think of bringing a flashlight down here in the mouth of hell?" Vera deadpans. "Of course not."

I feel Uriah's hand on my arm.

A beam of light illuminates the hallway.

Uriah's rare and boyish smile flashes against the light.

"There's a light on this rifle," he grins.

He pops the flashlight off the gun and beams it down the hallway. There's nothing but a long, endless stretch of passageway as far as the eye can see – an eternal stretch of darkness.

Under normal circumstances, I would be afraid. But I am so relieved to be out of Sky City – and away from Connor and the interrogation room – that I don't care. This is sweet relief.

"We'd better move quickly," Manny advises. "Mark my words – they're going to be coming fast."

"Or they'll have somebody waiting for us at the exit," Vera murmurs.

We move at a brisk pace – running and then jogging.

"How long is this passageway?" Uriah asks Arlene.

She holds up two fingers.

"Two *miles*?" Vera exclaims. "Wow."

"Sky City really *is* the ultimate doomsday bunker," I say. "They're prepared for anything."

"How could Unite go rotten, though?" Elle asks. "I mean, Unite was started during World War Two, right? Omega must have infiltrated before the EMP to get control of the entire base."

"It was a pretense, all of it," Colonel Rivera grumbles. "A ruse to get their sticky fingers on the militia's secrets. They've been bad for a long time – that's my suspicion, anyway. A very long time – if not from the very beginning. Killing Arlene was their way of getting rid of a woman who was about to tell Cassidy – and the rest of her team – that Unite couldn't be trusted."

There is a long pause.

"But why not just capture Arlene, like the rest of us? If this whole base is Omega, why try to assassinate her at all?" Vera points out.

"My guess is that not everyone here is working for Omega," Rivera replies. "I would be surprised if the entire population of Sky City was aware that we are imprisoned down here. The corruption runs deep, but Alan's attempt to kill Arlene could be something more sinister. He may have had orders from someone else. We'll never know because he's dead."

I ask, "What tipped you off, Arlene? After all this time?"

Arlene is nothing but a shadow in the darkness.

Her voice is a breathy whisper – barely there:

"They wouldn't destroy the insurgency base. I knew something was off, so I asked questions. And they shut me out." She shrugs. "Alan White tried to kill me. I don't why he waited so long to try...I just don't understand."

She stops, overwhelmed. The effort to speak must be very painful.

"What happens when we get to the end of this tunnel?" Vera asks. "We had an escape plan – but what then? We're hundreds of miles away from the valley. We're in the high mountains, for god's sake. There's no food, no water. Just wilderness."

I say nothing for a long time, because I *have* thought of what we will have to do to survive. There is nothing for us in the high mountains – no shelter, no food, no friendly forces. We are weak – all of us. We need backup. We need a way to communicate with Monterey, to warn Chris and the Pacific Northwest Alliance that Sky City is poisonous – that they are using their base to collect information from the militias.

Such a lie, I think, bitter. *Omega will pay for this.*

"We only have one option," I say.

I look at Colonel Rivera.

"We have to take out the insurgency base."

There is a long pause.

"What do we really know about this insurgency camp, anyway?" Vera points out. "Technically, *we're* insurgents. Insurgents fight against an established regime. That would be us *now*."

"They're insurgents because they've been training spies to infiltrate and destroy the structure of rebellion in the states for years," Rivera explains. "They still do the same thing. The rest of their forces have just finally invaded."

I look into the darkness.

I guess we know what we need to do.

Chapter Ten

"Is this really about doing the right thing, Cassidy?" *Chris asks me.*

We are in Monterey. The streets are smoking, littered with rubble. Andrew is in the hospital. Harry is in our custody. I am bloody, battered and bruised.

Sophia is dead. My friend. The girl who was like my sister.

I stand just outside the medical building in downtown Monterey.

"Of course," I say. "All of this – fighting and negotiating and losing people we love. It's all because we're doing the right thing. People who do the right thing have to sacrifice everything."

"You're angry with Omega," Chris replies.

"Of course I am," I say. "Aren't you?"

"Yes. Just remember. Don't let blind hatred take over. Ever."

I shake my head.

"All I'm asking for you to do is call for a military execution of Harry Lydell," I say. "He's earned that, don't you think?"

"Of course he has. But I also remember a girl who stopped me from killing Harry in the middle of the forest," he replies. "She wanted me to exercise humanity. To be fair."

"Harry is a killer," I say. "He doesn't deserve mercy anymore. He's earned a death sentence."

I am burning with anger. I am hurt, horrified. My best friend is dead – turned to betrayal by a man who we both once considered a good friend. I want him dead. I want Omega wiped off the face of the earth.

"I know that," Chris replies. He touches my cheek. "Harry will be executed. But he has to be interrogated first. He's valuable. He knows things about Omega that we don't."

I look at the smoldering remains of Monterey.

The dead bodies in the streets. The distant howl of sirens.

"Harry will be executed," he goes on. "But I don't want you to ever kill out of hatred. Killing in self-defense is one thing – killing for vengeance is entirely another."

"You kill people all the time," I shoot back, angry. "You've killed people for a decade. You're a SEAL. That's what you're trained for."

"I'm trained to protect," Chris answers, never wavering. "I'm trained to eliminate those people who would hurt my family, and my country. Anything beyond that is wrong." He shakes his head. "I just don't want you to get used to killing, Cassidy. You're better than that."

I rest my hands on my hips.

"I hate killing," I say. "But I hate Omega more."

A cool gust of wind blows Chris's hair into his face.

"We do what we have to so that we can survive," *Chris tells me. "We don't do it for any other reason than to* *protect and serve."*

I turn away from him, angry, unshed tears spilling *onto my cheeks.*

"This isn't just about survival anymore," I say. "This *is about revenge."*

*

It is all darkness. We eat what little rations Elle scavenged from the cellblock guards and pray that it will be enough to get us out of the tunnel. It stretches on for an eternity. We move as quickly as we can, knowing that Sky City and Unite will pursue us relentlessly – because with us is their dirty little secret. The secret that they are nothing more than another vitriolic head of Omega.

Another strain of the infection.

Harry was right, I think. *Omega is everywhere.*

The thought is terrifying – especially in a dark tunnel – so I push it away. I keep a firm grip on Uriah's arm as we navigate through the passage, only a single beam of light between us.

I am tired, underfed. I am afraid.

But I keep going. I tell myself that I am tougher than anything Omega can throw at me, and I repeat that over and over again until I believe it. Thankfully, we are moving fast enough that I don't have time to dwell on negative thoughts or pain. Arlene is doing well. She seems to have regained a little strength with the rush of adrenaline she utilized to escape the prison block.

"So, the insurgency camp," Vera says at last. "You want to take it over?"

"Yes," I reply.

"Just us."

"Just us and a dog," Elle corrects. "Don't forget Bravo."

"Right. Us and a *dog*," Vera huffs. "Cassidy, I know what you're thinking – and it's a good plan, really – but we can't. We don't have enough weapons or manpower. We've got nothing."

"What else are we supposed to do, then?" I ask. "Hide out in the woods and freeze to death? There's nothing out here, Vera. These are the high mountains, and it's November. It's *cold*. We'll die."

There is a long silence.

"Do you remember when I asked you to take out the insurgency camp in exchange for recruits, Hart?" Colonel Rivera suddenly asks.

"Yeah," I say. "What about it?"

"I asked you because Sky City wouldn't do it." He heaves a sigh. "We know why now. Sky City has been protecting the camp this whole time. When you came in for recruits, and when I asked you to complete that mission and trade recruits for it – it would have disrupted their operation. Blown their cover. Suddenly too many people would know what was really going on."

"So they tried to kill us all," Manny replies. "In all honesty, that's not very original. I could have seen that coming a mile away."

Arlene says nothing.

I imagine it must be quite a blow, knowing that the organization that you've devoted most of your life to is completely corrupt.

Talk about having a bad day.

"So what now?" Vera says. "We know their secret. We've got to tell someone."

I press my lips together.

"Exactly," I say. "Which is why we've got to get to the insurgency camp."

"Because *they'll* welcome us with open arms," Vera remarks.

"Because they'll have radios," I reply. "And weapons."

"Um, hello," Elle interjects. "It's an *insurgency training camp*. Everyone there is going to be *very* dangerous."

"We're more dangerous," I state. "Because we're desperate."

No one argues with that, and we drop the subject for a moment.

It seems to take forever, but eventually we reach the end of the passage. I see a light. Faint, far away. But it is there, and is enough.

"Is that sunshine?" Elle asks.

We all hesitate.

Is it?

Uriah flicks off the flashlight. Raw, natural sunlight fills the end of the black passage, like water spilling across a pool of ink. We move toward it. As we get closer, my eyes water. I shield them with my arm, coming up on what looks like a narrow slit. I squeeze through the space and step onto rock. I smell mountain dirt, I taste fresh air. I look up, and I see blue sky. I feel the frigid temperatures of the November weather.

"We're out," I say.

And then I grab the wall, because I'm standing on the edge of a very tall cliff.

"Whoa," I warn. "Be careful."

The tunnel literally empties onto the side of a granite cliff. A three-hundred-foot drop spins between the forest floor and me. I see miles of high, snow-dusted peaks surrounding us in every direction. Where we are, it is all rock and open plains. The defined line of a forest lies ahead, about two miles away.

"What are we supposed to do then?" Vera asks. "Climb down?"

There's no footpath, no trail. Just a sheer cliff.

"I'm assuming this is the *emergency* exit," Uriah says. "This access tunnel looks a little unfinished."

I look at him, and he grins.

"Anybody here good at rock climbing?" I ask.

"I am," Elle volunteers. "But Bravo might need some help."

The dog waits in the shadow of the tunnel, as if sensing the fact that whatever is about to happen isn't going to be a fun experience for him.

Sorry, dog. Not all things in life are fun.

About fifteen feet away, the cliff slopes at a slight angle.

"If we can get to that slope," I say, "we can slip down the rest of the cliff. Like a glissade."

"A rocky, sharp glissade," Vera mutters.

"It's better than being stuck up here until Omega finds us," I reply. I remove my jacket. "Let's make a rope, come on."

I am suddenly struck by the fear that Sky City, Unite – and all of Omega – will arrive at any moment. I mean – if we made it here this quickly, who's to say that they're not sending a search party into the woods right now. A kill squad?

I shiver.

Uriah, Elle, Arlene and Vera take off their nylon belts. We fasten them together, forming a long rope. It's not enough, though. We pool our jackets and cut them into long strips, elongating the length of the rope. I look at

Manny and Colonel Rivera. Of the two, Manny is the tallest, but Rivera is the strongest.

I hold up the end of the makeshift, pathetic escape rope.

Colonel Rivera says nothing. He just takes it. Any snide remark that he's thinking of making dies on his lips. Because he can't see any way out of this situation, either.

"Okay, Uriah," I say. "You go first. Then Arlene."

He nods.

Rivera drops the coat rope down the side of the cliff. It stops at the small ledge just before the slope. "Thirty years of military experience," he mumbles, "and I end up holding a rope made of jackets for a bunch of kids and a mutt."

Bravo growls softly.

"His name is Bravo," Elle retorts. "And he's a member of this team."

I smile, proud of Elle. Proud that she sticks up for her friend, proud that she's not afraid of Colonel Rivera. After everything, I have come to realize that despite all of his faults, he's just a man.

He puts one boot on the side of the tunnel wall as Uriah takes hold of the rope and slowly lowers himself over the edge, rappelling as gently as possible.

Rivera's arm muscles strain – but only a little. He is a big man. He can handle it. I hold my breath as Uriah slowly moves down, reaching the ledge. He looks up, then signals for Elle to move.

"Go on," I say.

She shows no fear as she grips the rope and rappels down the side of the cliff, as nimble as a cat. She lands near Uriah. "Okay, Arlene," I say. "You up for this?"

She whispers, "I don't have much of a choice, do I?"

Arlene closes her fingers around the rope and Colonel Rivera braces himself against the wall. It takes a long time for Arlene to get down the wall, but she makes it in one piece. "Manny," I say. "Take Bravo."

He doesn't argue.

"Okay, bomb dog," he announces. "You and me are taking the long way down. The long drop and the sudden stop." He tucks his arm around the dog and ties the rope around his furry waist. Malnutrition has worn Bravo thin.

He is the calmest dog I've ever seen. We slowly lower him over the side of the cliff. He stays still, as if sensing that his life depends on his cooperation.

Now that I think about it, he probably knows exactly what's going on.

When he reaches the ledge, Elle throws her arms around his neck. The bond between them makes me smile, and Bravo buries his nose into her chest.

After Vera makes it to the bottom, it's my turn.

"How will you get down?" I ask.

Rivera shrugs.

"Guess we'll figure that out."

I look at him, realizing that I am trusting my life to this man. This man, who I have seemed to hate for so long. And now we're on the same level, surviving, and he's helping me as much as I'm helping him.

I meet his gaze.

"Okay," I say.

I grip the long string of coats and slip down the side of the cliff. Uriah's strong arms close around my waist as I reach the bottom, and he lowers me down.

"Thanks," I say.

He opens his mouth to answer, but whatever he says is cut off by the sound of gunshot. It's funny – gunshots are such a familiar sound to me. I never expect myself to be startled by them anymore.

But today I am. Because the shot breaks the incredible stillness of the quiet mountain cliff. It comes from above us – from within the tunnel. Rivera stumbles to the side, wounded. He holds a hand to his chest, peering at the blood on his hand. He looks at me. I look at him.

He takes a grenade off his belt and throws it into the passageway. The grenade explodes, the blast ripping through Rivera.

And he falls.

Vera screams, horrified. His body flies past us, hitting the ground three hundred feet below with a heavy thud. I look away. Elle gasps. Arlene covers her mouth.

"MOVE!" Uriah yells. "They'll keep coming!"

I am numbed, shocked. I can't look away from the limp body on the forest floor, blood splattered out in every direction, limbs spread at odd, broken angles. I feel sick, like I'm stuck in some kind of nightmare.

Colonel Rivera...dead.

Uriah shakes me.

"Cassidy, come on!"

I don't know how I move, but I do. Uriah's voice is the only thing that draws me out of my horror. Everything seems to beat in slow motion as Elle, Vera, Manny and Arlene slide down the slope, skidding to the bottom of the cliff, landing in the dirt. I shove Bravo down the cliff. He growls and nips at me, but his resistance is only halfhearted. He gracefully guides his limber body down the slope, landing near Elle on all fours.

I cast a final glance behind me.

Sky City troopers – Omega – burst out of the tunnel. The first two don't realize that there is no path – just a cliff. They stumble. The first one slaps his head against the rock and falls in a twisted heap to the ground below, screaming. The second does the same.

The troopers behind them get smart.

They stand at the mouth of the tunnel and fire their weapons at us. Bullets ricochet off the rocks, echoing across the open landscape. But like most shooters, they don't realize that shooting downward is making their aim high, allowing us an escape.

Uriah slides his arm around my waist and I grab onto him, holding on for dear life. We slide down the rocky slope together. It's a painful ride, one that cuts up my legs and bruises my hips, but we land at the bottom without breaking any bones.

I roll over and over, cutting my face on sharp rock and shrubs. Bullets rain around me, hitting the dirt, missing me by inches. I scramble to my feet and rush to the two dead troopers on the ground.

"Cover me!" I yell to Uriah.

He knows exactly what I am doing. He fires at the troopers up above, standing in the mouth of the tunnel. I take the rifle from the first trooper. Vera is right behind me, collecting the weapons and ammo from the second, following my lead.

Once we've got everything, I cry, "RUN FOR IT! Peel back!"

We roll over each other's lines of defenses, like playing leapfrog in reverse, using the cover of gullies and rocks until we reach the cover of the tree line.

As we run, I pass the body of Colonel Rivera. I can't see his face – it's turned away from me, and I am grateful for that. I wouldn't want to see it, not after a fall like that. I see the blood of a bullet wound seeping through the back of his uniform, and despite everything that has happened between this man and me, I feel sadness. A great, gaping hole opens up in my heart.

The faster I run, the larger the hole becomes.

I do not feel sadness.

There is only anger.

There is only a desire for revenge.

Chapter Eleven

I understand what it is to be human. To be human is to make mistakes. To be human is to feel pain and loss. To be human is to be jealous, to be insecure. To be human is to be either supremely overconfident or to second guess every decision you make.

To be human is to feel, on an incredible level, the full agony of what it means to live. Of what it means to sacrifice the things that you want – and to lose the people you love the most.

As we walk through the forest, I think of Chris.

For ten years, all he did was fight and kill and lose people he loved. It was such a painful experience that his humanity was *removed*. He no longer felt anything. He was numb and tired. He existed – but that was all. And then came the EMP, the militias, and me.

And now, he says he is human again.

Me? I feel like I'm getting farther and farther away from my humanity.

Colonel Rivera's death has left me hollow inside. I don't feel sadness or betrayal. I don't even feel trauma. I am purely angry. I walk with my head tucked down, watching my steps as we trod through the woods, oblivious to the bitter cold. Frosty flakes of snow land on my face, sticking to my hair.

No one says a word.

We are all freezing, left with only thick wool shirts and pants, the remains of our coats left somewhere at the bottom of the cliff where Colonel Rivera had fallen to his death.

We follow Arlene's directions. According to her, we should be getting close to the insurgency camp. It's not too far away.

Of course, the whole idea of taking an insurgency camp down with just the few of us – and a dog – is insane. I know that it is impossible, and even with the four rifles that we took from Omega troopers, that's not enough to take down an entire camp. Besides, if Sky City and the insurgency camp have radio communications on a regular basis, I'm betting that they already know we're out here.

So what do we have to do?

Survive first. Get revenge second.

Patience, after all, is a virtue.

I scare myself a little, realizing how easily I shut off my emotions and focus on my tasks. My sole purpose right now is to keep my team alive, and I will do anything to make sure that we make it out of this situation without any more casualties.

Anything.

After hours of walking, the sun sets behind the peaks of the high peaks of Kings Canyon. It is freezing. The wind is cold, the snow is cold, the air is cold. I find a small rock formation in the forest as we bundle up beside it, using it as a windbreaker.

Together, we build a trench in the snow, laying down branches to provide insulation. We huddle up together, absorbing each other's body heat. Without that, we will all die. And, although it's not the most ideal survival method, we eat snow to keep hydrated. The ice melts in my mouth. It is a relief to not be thirsty anymore.

Bravo pushes his warm, furry body up against Elle. I envy their family unit. I wish Chris were here. I would wrap my arms around him and sleep soundly through the night.

I sit with my knees drawn against my chest, shivering.

Vera is curled into a tight ball, twigs in her hair, dirt on her face.

Uriah sits down beside me. His dark hair is crusted with ice. His skin is tight with cold, his coal-colored eyes glittering in the darkness.

"Do you remember when I tried to kiss you, and you basically punched me in the face and told me to back off?" he asks.

Despite everything, I laugh.

"Yeah," I reply. "On the way into Los Angeles, when we were rescuing Chris."

"You were right to do that," he goes on, watching the snowflakes fall. "When I first met you at Camp Freedom, your assertiveness is what drew me to you. You were stubborn and, sometimes, you were naïve. But you always had the best intentions, and that made you different."

He puts his arm around me, offering warmth.

I don't fight it. I press my cheek against his chest, thankful for his presence.

"We're friends now," he continues, sadness in his voice. "And I'm glad for that. But after Connor interrogated you...I wanted to kill him, Cassidy. More than you know. I didn't want to see you get hurt like that."

I say, "That's war, Uriah. People get hurt."

"But not you." He touches my hair. "I promised Chris I would keep you safe. I failed him."

"You failed no one." I close my eyes. "We're doing the best we can."

He leans his chin on my head, and I feel his heartbeat.

"We're going to make it," he says. "All of us."

I don't say what I am thinking.

I will make Omega pay for everything they've done. And if I die in the process...then so be it.

*

I wake to the cold, steel muzzle of a gun on my cheek. I don't dare move. I open my eyes, heart skyrocketing through my ribcage, fear surging through my veins. Uriah wakes, too, and his first instinct is the same as mine – fight or flight.

137

But, also like me, he realizes that it is better to remain still.

There are at least fifteen rifles aimed at our heads. One of them is still pressed against my cheek. I draw back, looking around us. It is early morning. Sunlight streams through the clumps of snow on the pines.

We are surrounded by men in black masks.

Omega insurgents, I think, panicked.

They wear earth-colored combat fatigues, their faces covered in black ski masks. I can only see their eyes. They are silent. I realize, too, that the rest of my team is awake, sitting, frozen. Vera looks at me, but she doesn't even twitch.

These enemies are so quiet – so ghostly – that it seems like we've walked into some kind of twilight zone terror show. It's dreamlike, unreal. I feel Uriah's heart beating through his chest. Every muscle in his body is taut.

"Who are you?" I ask at last, breaking the silence. "What do you want?"

No answer.

"Get up," one of them says. He is taller than the rest. I can see only his dark eyes. He motions with the tip of his rifle and I get to my feet, stiff and freezing. Uriah stands with me. "Put your weapons on the ground."

I slide my rifle off my shoulder, cradle it in my arms, and lower it into the snow. Uriah does the same, and so do Vera and Manny. Arlene is nearly blue in the face from the cold, blanched.

"Put your hands behind your heads," the man says.

His voice is deep, baritone.

I slowly move my hands behind my head, linking my fingers together. In the cold, they've stiffened so much that I can barely move them. I lick my lips.

We can't die like this, I think. *Not with Omega still out there.*

"WAIT!"

Boots crunch through the snow. Bushes rattle. A masked soldier walks into the circle of silent enemies. There is a raw, dangerous energy in the air. It is the scent of bloodlust – I know it well.

These men are here to kill. They *want* to kill.

"You can't kill these people," the newcomer says. "I know them."

The man who ordered us to put our hands up turns to him.

"What are you saying?" he asks.

"This is Cassidy Hart," the newcomer replies. "Her father is Frank."

The man – who is clearly in charge – lowers his rifle. He looks at me, then pulls off his ski mask. I gasp, because I recognize his face. Commander Jones – a militia commander who worked with my father and his militia, the Mountain Rangers. He is no longer big and burly – he is thin, worn. His face looks older than it did all that time ago, when I first arrived at Camp Freedom, before I joined the

National Guard. Before everything got so much more complicated.

"Commander?" Uriah raises his eyebrows.

"Lieutenant True," Commander Jones replies. His strong, powerful voice echoes off the trees. "Unbelievable. Vera Wright? And is that...Manny Costas?"

"The one and only," Manny replies, grinning crookedly. "Thought I was dead, did you?"

"Not so much dead as *gone*." Commander Jones seems amused at some inside joke, and I don't ask. "What are you doing in the high mountains? What happened to the National Guard – to Rivera? Last we heard, Commander Young was missing in action and you had pushed back Omega at the Battle of the Grapevine."

"God, how long have you been out of the loop?" Vera exclaims. "So much has happened since then! What are *you* doing out *here*?"

The man who identified us to Commander Jones pulls off his mask, and I recognize him, too. Desmond, the crazy field medic from Camp Freedom. This man once nursed me back to health after I'd been shot.

"Desmond?" I say.

I run forward and jump on him, wrapping him into a warm, desperate hug. He laughs heartily. His matted dreadlocks fall down his back. Beads and feathers are threaded through each dread. He looks tired, too. Like Commander Jones, his face has changed.

"It's good to see you, Cassidy," he replies, placing his hands on my shoulders. "A familiar face is not something you come across often. Not in times like these."

"You're still patching up the wounded?" Manny asks.

"And doing a damn good job, flyboy," Desmond replies.

"And the negative commentary has begun," Manny mutters.

I smile. Just like old times.

"What are you doing so high up in the hills?" I ask.

"I was about to ask you the same question," Desmond says. "What happened to ya'll?"

"Sky City," I reply. "That's what happened."

"So it's true." Commander Jones shakes his head. "We've heard rumors about that place. Didn't know it really existed. What was it like?"

"Crawling with Omega minions," Vera says. "It's completely infiltrated."

"We came to get more recruits," I explain, "but it was a trap. Omega has taken over Sky City. They're taken over everything."

Commander Jones looks stricken.

"I had no idea. Where's Commander Young, Cassidy?" he asks. "We're so out of touch – we have no more radios, no more—"

"What are you talking about, Jones?" Manny interrupts. "Camp Freedom has always had all the toys. What's going on?"

"We've had complications," Jones replies. "We're on our own at the moment." He gestures to the fifteen or so men surrounding us. "This is what remains of Frank Hart's Mountain Rangers."

"We call ourselves the Rogue Rangers, now," Desmond says, smiling.

"What *remains* of the Mountain Rangers?" I say, alarmed.

"Not long after Frank left Camp Freedom to represent the militias in Sacramento," Jones tells us, "we were attacked by insurgents. Omega mercenaries, I guess. They were well trained. The camp was hit hard. A lot of good people died." He pauses, and I can tell that there are many dark memories flashing through his mind. "We Rangers took it upon ourselves to track the insurgents back into the mountains, find out where their base was. We never found them. Instead, here we are. We're about ready to return home."

"You left Camp Freedom unprotected?" I demand.

"There's some military there. But Omega won't attack again." Commander Jones shrugs. "There's nothing left for them to take."

I run a hand through my hair, numb.

"How long have you been looking for the insurgents?" I ask.

"Two weeks – maybe three." He looks at Desmond. "We've lost some good men. The weather has been unforgiving. The insurgents aren't too nice, either."

I nod, understanding.

"Commander Young and the National Guard are in Monterey," I tell him. "We just pushed Omega off the West Coast – for now. We came to Sky City for recruits, but we now know that it was a lie."

"They were going to kill us," Vera clarifies. "All of us."

"You're lucky to be alive, then," Desmond comments.

"Colonel Rivera," I go on, "is dead."

"Such is the way of war," Commander Jones says gravely.

"We have no food or supplies, Commander," I continue. "We barely escaped Sky City with our lives. If you can help us, we'd appreciate it."

"You're our allies," Jones replies. "Of course we'll help you."

I motion to Arlene.

"She needs medical attention." I look at Desmond. "Can you help her?"

"Always a pleasure to serve a beautiful lady," Desmond answers, mock-bowing. He claps Uriah on the shoulder. "Good to see you again, young man."

Uriah doesn't seem deeply touched.

"Have you thought about the others?" he whispers in my ear.

"What do you mean?" I ask.

"The civilians at Camp Freedom. Who survived. Who didn't." He bites his lip, pensive. "The Young family – if they're still alive."

I exhale.

I say, "We have to stay focused."

Desmond kneels down by Arlene, taking out his medical kit.

"Well, look at you," he murmurs. "You get cut open with a knife, and on top of that, you're married to this old maniac." He grins at Manny. "You never told me you were a married man, Manny."

"You wouldn't have believed me," Manny shoots back.

"Of course not. I'm still wondering if this is some kind of psychedelic dream, man." Desmond chuckles and goes on about his business, checking Arlene, making sure her bandages are clean.

I face Commander Jones again.

"Jones," I say. "There's a lot you don't know. If you've been out of communication with the rest of the state, then you need to understand that Omega is very much *here*. They bombed Sacramento; my father – Frank – is missing in action."

Jones sits down on a fallen log.

"I'm sorry to hear that, Hart," he says. "Truly, I am. Your father was a good man."

"We don't know that he's dead," I reply, almost too quickly. "He could have survived the bombing. I don't know. I haven't had any communication with Sacramento for a couple of weeks."

Jones says nothing.

We both know what MIA really means.

"Chris Young is alive and well," I continue. "He's currently in Monterey, defending the West Coast. California has joined the Pacific Northwest Alliance, joining a coalition of Canada, Washington, Oregon and Mexico."

Jones rests his elbows on his knees.

He looks just as tired as me.

"The game is changing," he remarks. "So much is changing, so quickly. Little militias like us – we don't stand a chance now. Omega is getting stronger. Even the grassroots communities – the ones with the will to survive – are being picked apart by the insurgents in these mountains."

"I know about the insurgents," I say.

"You don't know *enough*," Jones argues. "These men – they've been trained to sniff out survivors and refugees in the mountains. They find them, and they kill them. They're like bloodhounds. They kill everyone, and they do it cruelly."

"Sounds like a party that needs to be shut down," Uriah comments.

"We've been searching for them for a long time," Jones says. "We keep losing their trail, and then we end up going back to camp."

I look at Arlene, fragile and weak, leaning against the rock for support as Desmond checks her out.

"That woman," I say, keeping my voice low, "is Arlene Costas – Manny's wife. She knows where the camp is."

Jones raises his eyebrows.

"And how did she come by that information?"

"She was working with Sky City – she's got a lot of information like that." I lean forward, whispering. "Commander, I want that insurgency camp gone. I'm talking wiped off the face of the earth."

He waits for me to continue.

"My team will help you take it out," I say. "First, because Omega needs to be destroyed, no matter where they are. And second, because I guarantee you their camp will have radios. We can use those to contact the Underground, and to warn Chris and the others in Monterey that Sky City is a trap."

Jones considers this.

After a long, heavy silence, he smiles.

"I like it," he says. "When do we start?"

I fold my hands together.

"Right away," I tell him. "Give me a rifle – a sniper rifle."

"Rumor has it there's no one in the militias that's a better shot then you," Commander Jones answers, grinning.

"That's not true," I reply. "Chris and Uriah run a close second."

I wink.

When I look back at Desmond, he is saying something in a quiet voice to Manny. Manny looks slightly concerned, but then he smiles, touching Arlene's cheek.

"Whatever you're scheming," Manny says, meeting my gaze. "I'm with you until the end."

"Me too," Elle adds. "And so is Bravo."

He wags his tail.

"Obviously we're all in," Vera snaps. "But first, food and water, please? We're all malnourished."

"Good point, Lieutenant," I say. "Food first. War second."

"You know what they say," Uriah tells me, deadpan. "Revenge is a dish best served cold."

"Who said anything about revenge?" I ask.

"It's written all over your face."

I think of my father. I think of Jeff Young. I think of Sophia Rodriguez. I think of Colonel Rivera, Nathaniel Mero and Angela Wright. All good people. All of them, dead. All of them, the fallen prey of Omega's predatory infection.

And I realize something.

I no longer feel anything – not sadness, not loss, not anger.

Just the powerful, fiery desire to destroy.

Chapter Twelve

We rest near the rock that sheltered us from the cold winds, supplied with jackets and food. The Rogue Rangers are mostly asleep, with just a few men on watch. Commander Jones, Desmond, Manny, Uriah, Vera and myself are gathered in a circle, eating stale jerky and crackers, courtesy of the Rangers. Arlene has a stick in her hand, and she is drawing a map in the snow.

"This," she says in her soft, injured voice, "is the insurgency camp. When Rivera and I were still working in Sky City, we were made to believe that it was located many miles away from us. This was a lie. One of the reasons that I suspected Unite and Sky City was infiltrated – and controlled – by Omega was because the information was full of holes." She sighs. "It took weeks, but we finally compiled a clear picture of the camp."

She draws a perfect square.

"It's not far from where we are. Maybe fifteen or twenty miles." She draws a circle around the square. "The camp is surrounded by a heavily guarded, electric fence. There are guard towers hidden in the trees. The camp itself is occupied by at least two or three hundred insurgents at all times. It's a hive, so to speak. They send insurgents into the woods on missions. As Commander Jones pointed out earlier, they sniff out survivors and refugees. They kill any resistance – even children."

She pauses to catch her breath, taking a sip of water from a canteen. She sits down on the log beside Manny. "To destroy this camp, you will have to draw the attention of the insurgents to a concentrated area, which will leave another area of the camp unguarded. This will allow someone to sneak through the back door and tear them apart from the inside."

"Uriah," I say. "You're good at distracting people."

He rolls his eyes.

"I can take a hint," he replies, smirking.

"Uriah can take some of your men on the east side of the camp," I say, touching the corner of Arlene's drawing with the toe of my boot. "He can distract them. I'll take a team through the back door. Getting through the fence shouldn't be a problem. I'll need snipers covering our advance." I look around. "You have snipers here, Jones?"

"I've got three," he shrugs. "They're not as good as you or your team, but they're accurate enough when it comes to shooting things up."

I nod.

"Good." I draw a line around the back of the camp. "If there's five hundred insurgents inside, we're going to need to blow the whole lid off the camp. We need explosives. Bombs. Semi-automatic weapons." I look up at Jones. "What kind of weapons do you have?"

"Some rifles, AKs." He folds his hands together. "RPGs, land mines, grenades. We've got a lot of toys. Every time we hunt for these suckers, we come well-prepared."

"That's what I like to hear," I say, smiling. "I want this camp in flames. We'll smoke them out, and force them to come to us."

Arlene leans forward and draws a long, curved line along the back of the camp drawing. "There's a large mountain directly behind the camp," she explains. "They have no escape. If you could force them forward, you could drive them straight into our waiting arms."

"That's what I'm saying," I reply. "We'll give them two options: stay in the camp and burn, or run out the front door and get shot." I lift my shoulders. "Either way, we win."

I look at the map.

How would Chris handle this? I ask myself. *Would he cage them in? Would he force them out?*

"Remember," Manny interrupts, "that we're after their radio equipment. Without that, we can't contact Monterey – or the Underground – to warn them about Sky City. We'll be stuck in the hills for a long, long time."

"Good point. We want to take down the camp, but we don't want to raze it to the ground," I say. "Our priority is to make that call to Monterey. To warn them."

Vera nods, her icy-blue eyes glued to the crude map in the snow.

"How can we blow the lid off the camp without destroying the radio equipment?" she asks. "I mean, technically speaking, that's not really doable."

I think about this before answering.

"We'll do the best we can," I say. "At the very least, we can commandeer some vehicles and use them to get out of the mountains. No matter what happens, taking down this camp will be a good thing for everybody."

Nobody argues with that.

"I've got one last question, Commander," Desmond announces. "If things go south...if we can't pull this off for any number of reasons..." He looks at me. "What then? Do we peace out or surrender or something?"

"Peace out?" Manny grumbles. "Only cowards *peace out.*"

"Hey," I interject. "That's not a bad question. If things go south, we'll retreat and head back to Camp Freedom with Commander Jones and the Rangers. That's our only alternative."

"We should start moving, then," Jones says. "It will take us a couple of days to reach the camp, if Arlene's coordinates are correct."

"Of course they're correct," Arlene replies, obviously insulted. "I don't make stupid mistakes."

Desmond raises his eyebrows, looks at me, and points at Manny.

I laugh and stand up.

"Okay," I say. "We have a plan. Let's go."

"This better work," Vera comments.

"It will," I say. "It has to."

In my heart, I have no doubt that I'm right.

*

I'm sitting outside on the front steps of the warehouse in downtown Monterey, California. Chris is inside, talking to someone. Nobody has arrived yet, so I'm just waiting. Down the street, near an old antique shop, a dead body is lying in the gutter. It's one of our men. He's young – can't be older than twenty. His eyes are wide open, staring at the sky.

I rise from the steps and walk toward him, treading softly. When I reach him, I see that the left side of his face is no longer there. It's been burned off. All that is left is a mass of tissue and white bone. I look at his uniform. The patch above his breast pocket says **PETERSON.** *I take a step back, staring.*

I have never seen death in a setting that is not hectic. Men and women have died around me on multiple battlefields, but this is different. This is still, quiet. This is the deep and resounding reminder that our mortality is our biggest weakness.

I turn away from the dead soldier and walk back to the warehouse. I want to tell someone to go take Peterson's body and bury it, but I know that will be done soon. All of the bodies will be buried somewhere. The Battle of Monterey will be memorialized. And, if God is willing, a hundred years from now, people will remember the sacrifices of these poor young boys.

"Cassidy, you can come in if you want," Chris says, standing in the doorway.

He looks sad. Knowing.

"Coming," I tell him.

I stand up.

And I know in that moment that this war is far from over.

It has only just begun.

*

We have been moving toward the insurgency base for an entire day now, camping only for a few hours in the darkness of night to rest. The second day, we are only ten miles away from the camp.

There is not a lot of chitchat. No talking. Everyone is somber, quiet. We are tired, we are cold. We are hungry and homesick. But we keep pressing on.

I am walking toward the front of the group. We move in formation, ghosting through the woods as quietly as we can. I keep my rifle handy. My hand often rests on my belt, reaching for my knife – but it's not there.

I feel a pang of sadness. That knife was special to me, a gift from Jeff Young.

And now it's probably been thrown away somewhere in Sky City.

That thought just makes me angrier, and I find myself stomping through the woods, ahead of the rest of the group. I reach the crest of a hill. It has finally stopped snowing, and sunlight is glowing through the dark clouds gathering over the tips of the high mountains.

"It'll snow again soon," Manny gathers. "And I sure don't want to be the one stuck out in the blizzard."

"What? Being a snowman has no appeal to you?" I ask.

"No. I'd rather maintain my current body temperature." He helps Arlene up the hill. We look over the scenery. We have dropped at least two thousand feet in elevation. There are more trees here, and the terrain is not as choppy – or as rocky.

"Onward, folks," I say.

I keep moving. My boots knock the snow off the top of a patch of sweet-smelling bear clover. It reminds me of my family cabin, and I get a flash of pleasant childhood memories. I actually smile.

A gunshot zings right by my head.

The sound of the bullet makes my ears ring. I duck, hitting the ground on my palms. The bullet hits a tree behind me, leaving a hole in the bark. Up ahead, I see a flicker of movement. Dark cloth and rustling leaves.

"What was that!?" Vera yells.

I run. I don't stop to talk or think. I just follow the flicker in the forest, sprinting as fast as I can. My muscles burn, sweat slides down my forehead. I don't care. I can see the movement of the enemy up ahead. Whoever attacked us is quiet and clever – but not clever enough. His fear of being caught is making him noisy – panicked.

I am faster than he is. I am quieter. I am angrier.

I zigzag between trees and plow through dormant beds of fern. I am sure that Uriah and most of the Rangers are right behind me, but I don't stop to look. I am closing in on my target. I can see boots, dark hair and black clothing. I see the flash of a rifle in the sunlight.

I run at an angle. I am moving faster than he is. Our paths intersect and I slam into him. We tumble over and over again, hitting the ground. I taste blood in my mouth, bitter and metallic. I put my knee on his chest and whip my rifle around. I hold it parallel against his throat, pressing his neck against the ground.

"Don't move," I warn.

I look at his face. He is young. Very young. He looks like a child. There is still baby fat in his cheeks, his clear blue eyes glittering against the snow.

Uriah catches up to us a few seconds later.

"Damn, you're fast, Cassidy," he heaves, kneeling beside me. He trains the muzzle of his rifle on the boy's head. "That's right. You move, you get a bullet in your skull. Understand?"

I take my knee off the boy's chest and sling my rifle into my arms.

He looks terrified. His pale cheeks are flushed. I look at his uniform. Black. A red band is tied around his arm. I've never seen something like that before.

"What's this for?" I ask the boy, pulling on the band.

He doesn't answer. He just lies there, breathing hard, glaring at me.

Eventually, the rest of the group pushes through the woods. Jones rests his rifle on his shoulder, shaking his head.

"He looks like a child," he remarks.

"He is," I say. "His uniform has no markings. Just the red band."

"Insurgency," Desmond says. "They wear the red bands. It's supposed to signify blood and death – or something messed up like that. It's not cool." He shakes his head. "Poor kid. Why can't these people just take a chill pill and leave us alone?"

No one replies.

"Messed up," Desmond mutters.

"How old are you?" I ask the boy, kneeling beside him.

He still says nothing.

"Do you speak English?' I ask.

I look at Manny.

"What do you think?" I say.

"I think he's a scout," he replies. "And we can't let him go."

"So we kill him," Elle states.

Commander Jones raises one eyebrow.

"I see your niece is no stranger to taking another man's life," he remarks, glancing at Manny. "Is that something she learned from you?"

"I learned on my own, actually," Elle retorts. "I'm just saying what everybody's thinking. We can't let him go – he'll tell the insurgents that we're coming."

I ponder this.

Elle is right, of course. Not only did he try to kill me, he will alert the insurgents at the base that we are on our way to torch their camp.

"We'll keep him alive," I say. "For now."

"That's a waste of energy and resources—" Vera begins, but I cut her off, an idea forming in my head.

"If he doesn't talk, we'll make him talk." I shrug.

He swallows.

I think of Arlene, how she almost died - how I was tortured, over and over again. Why should I show any mercy to an Omega insurgent?

Why should I be any different?

Still, nothing.

I stand up and press my boot against his throat. No one says anything, nobody tries to stop me. Why should they? I press hard enough to make him cough and sputter. His face turns a pale shade of purple.

"Are there other scouts out here?" I ask. "Has anyone else seen us? How long have you been following us?"

He chokes and struggles against my boot, but I have the leverage. I keep him down. "Cassidy…" Uriah begins, but I give him a look.

He backs down.

"Tell me what you know, or I will kill you," I say.

"You are militia," the boy says at last. His voice is heavily accented. "What is your name?"

I lift my rifle into my shoulder.

"My name is Cassidy Hart," I say, peering through the sights, centering them on his chest.

There is so much fear in his eyes. Pure terror.

"No!" he begs. "Please, no! Don't kill me, please!"

"Why should I let you live?" I ask, never moving. "You tried to kill me."

"I was only doing my job, Fraulein."

I pause.

"You're German," I say.

"Please," he pants, holding his arms up. "When I was very young, Omega brought me here. Slave trade. Human trafficking, you Americans call it. I have trained in these mountains since I was a child, waiting for the right moment to strike."

I feel a pang of sadness.

A poor, innocent boy, brought overseas by Omega years ago, in preparation for the EMP and invasion.

"And when does Omega think the right time to strike actually *is*?" I ask.

"Now," he replies. A strange smile spreads across his lips.

"Are there any other scouts in these woods?"

"Just me, Fraulein. Just me."

I don't believe him.

"How many men are at your camp?" I ask.

"Thousands."

"You're lying." I press the cold, steel muzzle of my rifle in the center of his rifle. "Lie to me one more time. I dare you."

He goes still.

"How *many*?" I demand.

"Two hundred." He blanches. "Fraulein, you stand no chance against us with a force this small."

"Yes, we do, actually." I take the rifle from my shoulder and sling it across my back. "You're going to help us, blondie."

I step aside and Uriah grabs the kid by the scruff of the neck, gathering all his weapons.

"Exactly how is the string bean going to help us take down the camp?" Vera asks. "I don't think he could figure out how to hunt a deer, let alone a person. He missed you by a mile."

"Trust me," I reply. "He *will* help us."

I turn to the boy, his hands now tied in front of him.

"You got a name, kid?" I ask.

He glares at me once again.

"Have it your way." I shrug. "Okay, listen up, people. We're closing in on the camp. We can assume that there are more scouts like Doctor Obvious over here, so we need to keep a low profile. No more talking. I want silence."

I gauge the position of the sun. "It'll be dark in a couple of hours. We need to move quickly."

"And how does sunshine factor into all this?" Uriah asks, shoving the boy toward me. "He's just dead weight."

"We'll use him to draw the insurgents out of the camp," I say.

In my mind, I see the pieces of an elaborate puzzle coming together. I feel a jolt of electricity, and I realize that I'm *excited*. Scared to death? Sure. But excited. The rush of going on a mission is a thrill ride like no other.

My name is Cassidy Hart, I think. *I am vengeance.*

Chapter Thirteen

It is the dead of night. I lay prone on the crest of a hill, looking at a scene that will probably never fade from my memory. The insurgency camp is nestled snugly against the side of a mountain peak. It is hidden in the shadow of a cliff, invisible from the air. From my vantage point, it is little more than a collection of barracks with a chain link fence around it. Barbed wire tops the fence, and outside that, another layer of fencing surrounds the perimeter. The electric fence.

Dark, dangerous thunderheads are closing fast, blotting out the moonlight. It is difficult to see anything, but dim, orange lights around the camp allow me to make out shapes and movement.

I have my rifle tucked into my shoulder, keeping my eyes on the camp through the scope. I feel oddly comfortable like this. Calm. It is what I am used to – it's what I know. Uriah lies prone beside me, silent. There are Rogue Rangers all around us, hidden in the trees.

There are only two guard towers in camp – both in the front. Because there is nothing but a rock wall behind the camp, no one is really watching that area of the fence.

"You think this will work?" Uriah whispers.

"It's the best I've got," I reply.

A muddy road curves to the entrance of the camp. There's a roadblock and checkpoint there. Cement blocks are set up around the camp, too – probably to keep vehicles from charging through the gates, I guess. The barracks are quiet tonight. Only one building is lit from the inside, flickering with orange lamplight.

"These suckers are quiet," Uriah says.

"And to think that they've been training insurgents for at least two decades," I reply. "Kind of makes me sick."

"It makes all of us sick."

I sweep the trees, then return my focus to the muddy road that curves toward the camp entrance. I watch carefully as a shadowy figure starts walking down the road. I keep my sights trained on his head.

Please let this work, I pray.

The figure walking toward the camp is the boy that we captured earlier today. Stripped of his weapons, I told him to march into camp and tell the guards at the first checkpoint that a huge force of militia soldiers are coming up the road. The purpose, of course, is to draw the insurgents out of their barracks and send them on a wild goose chase while we take the camp. Their numbers will be cut in half, and when the rest of the insurgents return from their fruitless mission, we'll be waiting.

But it all depends on whether or not the scout follows through.

"If you do anything suspicious – anything that even slightly *looks wrong,"* I warned him earlier, *"I will shoot you."* I motioned to Uriah, Vera and myself. *"We are all*

snipers. We can kill you from a mile away. You understand?
If you alert them to our presence, we will take you out."

He nodded then, trembling.

"You know what to say. Tell them you were
captured by scouts, that you escaped," I went on. "Tell them
you barely escaped with your life. Tell them that we're
coming for the camp, and they should cut us off on the
mountain roads, below the camp."

He nodded again.

"Remember," I continued, tapping my rifle. "I hold
your life in my hands. Don't mess this up."

I have no regrets. I am not sorry for threatening
the boy – he's not innocent. Yes, he was trained to kill, and
he didn't have any choice. But the fact remains that,
regardless of how he became the bad guy, he *is* the bad
guy. And because of that, I won't cut him any slack.

I don't pity the enemy. I pity their victims.

I keep my sights trained on the scout's head as he
approaches the front gate. There is a flurry of activity at
the checkpoint. Omega guards – dressed in the same,
unmarked black uniform as the scout – emerge from
within the gates to greet their missing man. There is
talking. I watch the scout's face. It's difficult to discern
what he's saying, but it looks like it's going well.

He waves his arms and gestures down the road.

The guards run back into the camp. The scout
lingers there for a second, looking up into the hills. He
knows that there are snipers watching the camp. He also

knows that the second he makes a break for it, I will shoot him.

There is a moment of hesitation on his part.

He stands at the gate, clearly tempted to go inside. I know what he is thinking – that if he makes a mad dash for the gate, he will get away with it. That we won't shoot him, that he'll tell the insurgents not to leave the compound, and that we'll all die out here.

My finger hovers over the trigger of my rifle.

I am more than capable of following through with my threat.

And then he turns away from the camp and slinks back into the shadows, into the waiting arms of the militia hidden in the trees. I release a tense breath.

"That was fun," Uriah whispers, deadpan.

"I had a feeling he wanted to live," I reply.

The camp buzzes with activity. Troops pour out of the barracks. They arm up, get in their vehicles and form a convoy. There are maybe one hundred men deploying into the woods. The guards open the front gates and the convoy pulls out. They grind onto the gravelly, muddy road and rumble through the forest.

If the guards at the entrance have noticed that the German scout disappeared again, they don't show it. They don't seem to care.

I close my eyes.

Without radios to communicate with each other, the Rogue Rangers and the rest of my team have to rely on instinct to implement the plan. We are supposed to wait twenty minutes before we attack the camp, giving us enough time to get inside, cut down the insurgents and close the camp up before the troops in the convoy come back.

We'll be waiting for them, then.

Tick, tock.

I count the minutes under my breath, stiff from lying on my stomach, tired. I open a canteen and take a drink of water. Uriah is the only sniper close enough to me to actually talk to. Vera is elsewhere. Manny is with Elle and Arlene.

"Twenty minutes," Uriah says at last.

I nod.

I hope everyone else is on the same clock that we are. I watch the front entrance, counting down.

Whoosh.

I hear the distinct sound of an RPG being launched. It sounds like someone popping a lid off a metal can. It echoes through the forest, streaking toward the camp. The RPG hits the front gate and rips the metal apart. The detonation sends up a blaze of flames and shrapnel. Bits of barbed wire and chain link fencing flies everywhere. I can feel the heat from the blaze on my face.

The ground shakes.

Another RPG whistles through the air and hits the corner of the camp, smashing into the base of the guard tower. The tall structure collapses on itself. The guards inside try to throw themselves out of the building as it falls, but they land in a strangled heap on the ground, bones broken, skin burned.

The entrance has been blasted wide open.

I lean into my gun and peer through the optics. Insurgents surge into the camp from within the barracks, armed. They cannot see us, but they know we are there. We have the advantage, and I am proud of that.

I systematically pick off as many guards as I can. Gunshots ring through the air, dulling my sense of hearing. Everything becomes a loud, exploding blur. Uriah takes shots beside me, too. The Rogue Rangers let loose with everything they've got – guerilla warfare in its most impressive form.

I see an Omega insurgent running toward cover at the corner of the camp, taking shelter behind the fallen guard tower. Hitting a target that is moving quickly is one of the more difficult aspects of being a sniper. I follow him with my rifle, leading the target in my sights. I squeeze the trigger and my bullet slices through the air, dropping him instantly.

Aim small, miss small, I think. *That's what Chris always says.*

And, as always, Chris is right. The smaller I make my targets, the less room there is for me to miss. If I aim for a two-inch square, I might miss by a couple of inches, but I will still hit my target.

It's these little tips and tricks that make my job interesting.

If you can call this a job.

Eventually, the insurgents in the camp wise up. They take cover behind the buildings. They stop running out into the open, realizing that a hidden force surrounds them. I desperately want to use the remainder of our RPGs to blow up the barracks and destroy their cover, but I keep our goal in mind: preserve the radios!

We have no way of knowing which building the radios are in – or if there *are* any – so we'll need to make sure all of them survive this firefight.

"It's time to go down on foot," I tell Uriah.

"You sure?" he asks.

I shrug.

What else are we supposed to do? We've reached a stalemate. The only thing left is to walk through those doors and finish this thing.

Uriah doesn't argue. I rise from my spot and start moving down the hill. My movement is a signal to the rest of the Rangers hidden in the forest that it's time to rush the camp. I move as quickly as possible.

There is a cessation of fire as we move.

The insurgents don't shoot. We don't shoot.

There is silence. I stop near the corner of the entrance, nervous about breaking cover. I look at Uriah. The smoldering flames of the RPGs dance on the guard tower and a few overturned Omega vehicles.

"If I didn't know any better," Uriah says, panting. "I'd say we were walking right into the gates of hell."

I roll my eyes.

"So dramatic," I reply.

And that burst of sarcasm gives me the confidence to break cover. The Rangers cover me as I advance through the gate, stepping over the fiery threshold of the entrance. I shoot as I move, zigzagging, never pausing, never making myself a stationary target.

Constant movement will keep me alive. Yet another trick I've learned.

Uriah is right behind me, and suddenly the camp is being flooded with the Rangers. I slide behind an Omega pickup. Bullets ping off the roof as I kneel down, catching my breath. Sweat slides down my back, sticking my shirt and jacket to my skin.

I don't even feel the cold weather anymore.

Bright bursts of muzzle fire light up the night, bubbles of illumination against the dark mountainside. It is a familiar situation for me, but I would rather be fighting side by side with Chris.

Focus, focus, I remind myself

I poke the muzzle of my gun over the tip of the pickup and take several shots at insurgents that are stupid enough to break cover. About ten of them are charging forward between two barracks, guns blazing, screaming bloody murder. There is a type of madness in their eyes, desperation. They don't seem to care that their push is suicidal – from the look on their faces, they're almost welcoming it.

I take out the first two men at the front of the group. They hit the ground. Their bodies are trampled by the rest of their group. The Rangers open fire on them and raze the squad to the ground, until there is only one man left alive.

He picks up a gun from one of the fallen and screams at us. I can't understand what he's saying – there is too much noise and gunfire. As he runs, I'm struck by the focus. He runs without faltering, without stopping. He knows he is going to die. He doesn't even try to prolong his life by finding cover. He just runs, firing off shots in the direction of the militia.

Uriah kneels down – about twenty yards away from me – and shoots him. The force of the bullet knocks him backward. He hits the ground at a twisted angle, eyes wide open, blood trickling out of his mouth.

It's sad that someone so young would give themselves – body and soul – to a cause that has brought nothing but pain and cruelty to the world.

My sympathy is short-lived.

I move from cover to cover, slipping like a shadow between points, Uriah following right behind me. To the side of the camp, I see Manny bursting through the fence, guns blazing, a wild smile on his face. He charges inside, hollering. His flight cap is fastened around his head, tangled in his gray hair.

He looks crazy.

He swings around the corner of one of the barracks, taking out an insurgent who's creeping around the back.

"Come and get it, you bloody cowards!" Manny yells, laughing.

Uriah looks at me as if to say, *What are we going to do with him?*

I'm just glad he's on our side.

I check my left and right, ready to move from the corner of the front barracks to the next. An Omega trooper with dark skin and black eyes leaps from behind cover, grabs my shoulders and slams me against the wall before I can bring my weapon up. My head spins – not so much with pain but from familiarity. I remember being slammed against a wall on my first big guerilla mission with Chris and *Freedom Fighters.*

Déjà vu.

Only *this* time, neither Sophia or Chris is here to help me. I duck and spin around, bringing my rifle up to block a violent jab toward my face. The insurgent curses in a foreign language, scraping his fist against the metal of my gun, bloodying his knuckles.

I spin the gun around and shove it into his throat.

He stumbles backward, hitting the wall.

He tries to grab my gun, but it is attached to a sling that's strapped around my body, so I slam into him, inches from his face.

Gross.

I can smell his sweat. His meaty hands close around my body and he crunches me against him, squeezing the air from my lungs. Desperate for oxygen, I struggle against his iron grip, unable to grab my gun. My arms are pinned to my sides.

I have no hands, my legs are paralyzed by his weight, crushed between him and the wall. With no other options left, I sink my teeth into his cheek and bite as hard as I can. The taste of blood and flesh mingle in my mouth. It's disgusting.

He screams and drops me, grasping his cheek.

I spit and cough, gasping for breath.

He's enraged. He drops his hand. Blood and teeth marks scar his cheek. A piece of his cheek has been torn away. I shudder, feeling like a feral animal.

But his hesitation is his mistake.

Before I can grab my rifle or make a move to defend myself again, Uriah sprints across the camp, coming to my aid. He pops two rounds into my attacker's back. He looks down at his chest. He looks shocked, almost, to see the blood blossoming there. He looks at me. And then he falls forward, landing face first on the ground.

"Are you hurt?" Uriah asks, holding his hand out.

I take it, getting to my feet. My face is smeared with blood – thankfully, it's not my own. "I'm fine," I say.

I grab my rifle and turn back to the camp. It looks like we've taken down the defenses. Omega is running.

Elle and Bravo emerge from the border of the camp. Elle's got a small rifle in her hands, grease smudged across her face. Bravo trots beside her, calm and collected despite the gunfire and screams. Vera is not far behind them. She looks *angry*. A huge frown spreads across her face as she stalks toward Commander Jones and the Rangers.

I cross the length of the camp, joining the group.

It looks like the firefight is over.

"Seriously," Vera rants, turning to me. "That took way longer than it should have!"

"I think we did good, actually," I reply. "Calm down."

"Don't tell me to calm down. The rest of the insurgents are heading into the hills." She folds her arms across her chest. "They'll be back with help. We need to be ready for them."

"We will be," I say.

Dead insurgents are everywhere.

"And this is the downfall of man," Desmond murmurs, coming up behind me. "The killing."

"They've earned it," I say, cold.

"Yes," he agrees. "They have."

My ability to feel sadness for the enemy is gone. Their cruelty and evil have spread too far and injured too many people that I love. I no longer care about showing them mercy. I only care about showing them revenge.

"Human beings are the only species on Earth that kill each other like this" Desmond says slowly, his eyes sad. "Here we are, supposedly smarter than any other creature in the universe. And look what we do to each other. We tear each other apart."

I look at Elle. She's so young, yet she watches the entire thing with an expression of stone. A child her age shouldn't be so used to killing. She should be going to high school or wondering who's going to take her to prom.

Normal things.

Yet here we are, victims of a cruel world.

"This is life, now," I say. "We do what we have to do."

"I know," Desmond sighs. "But it's not right."

"No," I reply. "But Omega started this thing – and we'll be the ones to finish it."

Vera suddenly looks calm.

"Yeah," she agrees. "We will."

*

I stand inside the main building of the insurgency camp. We have set fire to the barracks. A plume of thick, black smoke rises into the air, obscuring the moonlight.

The main building is filthy. It's a wide, squat room with dirty windows. Maps are pinned to every wall. The insurgents have been tracking militia movements. I trace my finger on a red circle drawn around two letters: CF.

"Camp Freedom," I say aloud.

"Yes, they've been busy," Desmond comments, standing in the center of the room, taking in the atmosphere. Tables are littered with trash. Vile pictures and crude messages written in foreign languages are taped to the wall.

It looks more like a gang hideout than it does an insurgency headquarters.

But I remember what the German scout said – about how children were trafficked from foreign countries and brought here to train. I would expect nothing less from people who dabble in human slavery.

In the back of the room, away from the window, is a radio. It's old, outdated. It's got a handheld receiver and a big speaker. But it's something.

"I'm almost afraid to touch it," I remark. "What if it's keyed into Omega airwaves?"

Vera says, "If Andrew were here, he could figure it out for us."

There is sadness in her voice. I know she misses Andrew – we all do, honestly. I stick my head out the door. "Manny!" I call.

I wait. The tension mounts.

The Omega troops will be returning any time. The Rogue Rangers are out on the road, ready to intercept the convoy while we try to get the radio to work.

Manny walks inside with Arlene.

She is looking better. Tired, but better.

"Arlene," I say. "You know more about radios than anybody else."

She nods. No reason to deny it. She's the best we've got, other than Andrew – and since he's in Monterey…we have to do what we have to do.

She picks up the receiver and looks at it.

"This is tuned into Omega frequencies," she says. "I'll find a new channel."

The distant sound of gunfire and detonations sends a rumble through the ground. "Better hurry," Manny advises. "We're about to have company."

And the countdown is on.

Vera scurries into the room, right behind Uriah.

"Have we sent a message yet?" she asks. "Please tell me you have."

"We're working on it," Manny replies. "Just keep your shirt on."

She huffs, annoyed. Uriah never leaves the doorway, peering into the darkness. "The Rangers can only hold back the reinforcement insurgents for so long. They'll hit the camp." He looks at me. "Let's get this over with."

I don't argue.

I pick up the receiver and close my eyes, choosing my words carefully.

"*Alpha One*," I say. "This is *Yankee One*. Mike Foxtrot. Mission is FUBAR. Priority EXFIL your AOR ASAP."

I take my finger off the transmit button. If anyone in the Underground is listening, they will relay this message to Chris, and he will know exactly what I'm talking about.

I repeat the message over and over until we have to leave.

The second wave of insurgents is nothing like the first. I am perched on top of the radio building, my rifle in my arms, prone. The Rogue Rangers have done a considerable amount of damage to the Omega convoy. Only four vehicles are left. The rest are smoldering in the woods, and I can hear the smattering of gunfire from here.

They are cleaning up, and they're doing it well.

The occasional insurgent breaks out of the cover of the woods, but Uriah and I take them out before they can even reach the fence line. I find it ironic that this place – which only an hour ago was a cesspool of Omega activity – is now ours.

"You know," Uriah says, kneeling beside me, "since we took out this camp, every hostile Omega force in this area is going to come after us – if they're not already."

"I know," I reply. "But we got the message out. That's all we can do."

"So what then?" he continues. "We just camp out in the woods? We can't wait here. Omega will come for the camp."

"We'll take their vehicles, weapons and food," I say. "And we'll leave."

Uriah considers this.

"So we'll go back to Camp Freedom with Commander Jones and the rest of the Rangers," he finishes. "It's going to be a chore, getting back to Monterey."

"I know," I reply. "But we'll just have to do the best we can."

Vera, Manny and Desmond are walking through the camp, overseeing the Rogue Rangers' foraging. The militia goes through each building, dragging out crates and boxes of food and supplies, piling them into the remaining Omega vehicles behind the camp.

We take an entire pickup load of ammunition and guns. When the insurgency advance is over, I throw my legs over the lip of the building and climb down the gutter pipe.

"Do you have everything?" I ask Desmond.

He looks up from a Humvee, dreads and feathers fluttering in the cold breeze.

"I've got enough medical supplies in here to last us for another couple of years," he answers. "This is an answer to prayer, man."

"Good." I squeeze his shoulder. "Well done, Desmond."

"Camp Freedom needs this," he mutters, sticking his head back inside the Humvee, rummaging through the equipment – rolls of bandages and bottles of antiseptic.

Elle is standing, her back against one of the last barracks, Bravo standing with his head against her knees. A somber expression is on her face. I walk over.

"You okay, Elle?" I ask.

Her crystal blue eyes flick up, meeting my gaze.

"Yes, Commander," she replies.

She continues staring into the distance. I follow her line of sight.

"What makes us the good guys?" Elle asks softly. "We kill just as much as the enemy."

I kneel down, scratching Bravo behind the ears.

"We kill in self-defense – not out of cruelty," I tell her.

"I've killed a lot of people, Commander," she replies, looking away. "They were all bad people, but still. I've done it. Over and over." She sighs. "I guess I just get a tired of it sometimes."

"I get tired of it, too," I tell her. "The killing. It's horrible."

"But it's necessary."

"It's only necessary in self-defense."

"So we have to kill others to keep ourselves from getting killed," Elle states.

"Yes."

"That's so...twisted."

"It is," I agree. "But *war* is twisted."

I touch her cheek, the one with the scar.

179

"Omega has taken everything from us," I tell her. "They're cruel. They're *evil*. If we have to take extreme measures, it's because they forced us to. This is our home. Don't ever forget that. This is *ours*. They have no business being here."

Elle nods.

And then she steps forward and slips her arms around my neck, leaning her chin against my shoulder. I am surprised by her display of emotion – but I am glad. I embrace her and kiss the top of her forehead.

I stand up, my arm around her petite shoulders. Omega has driven us to such desperate measures. We have done everything we can to preserve our humanity, but nothing can take away the fact that we are all killers now.

All of us.

Whether we like it or not.

*

We leave the insurgency camp in flames. We send out a couple of more coded messages on the radio before torching the last building. The blaze is huge, throwing orange firelight against the trees, reaching to the dark sky.

We commandeer five remaining Omega vehicles, packing them with supplies. I ride in the front seat of a pickup with Uriah. As we drive, wind begins howling through the trees.

"Storm's coming," Uriah murmurs.

"I hope we can make it back to Camp Freedom before it hits," I answer.

The inside of the truck is cold, but the cabin protects me from the wind – a luxury I'm grateful for. I'm exhausted. My head throbs, pulsating with the pain of stress. So much planning and strategizing – all of it, with the purpose of keeping my men alive is a lot of pressure.

I wish Chris were here to share the burden with me.

Even with Uriah and the rest of my friends here, I still feel alone.

I miss Sophia. I miss my father.

Things change, sunshine, I can hear Sophia saying. *We'll make it through.*

The roads through the mountains are steep, curving around cliffs, single-lane back roads hidden from sight. The headlights illuminate the black forest. We move slowly in the convoy, only four vehicles behind us.

I've got a map spread across my lap. It's one of a huge stack that I took from the insurgency headquarters, with dozens of Omega routes outlined in red throughout the hills. There's a lot of valuable information here that should be in the hands of the Pacific Northwest Alliance – and the rest of the militias.

"We're on track," I say, flicking the dash light on. I drag my finger over a marked route, cutting south through the mountains, emptying at a campground about forty miles away from Camp Freedom. "Just a few more miles, and we'll clear these trees and hit a real highway."

"Let's hope Omega isn't waiting for us," he replies.

Yeah. Let's hope.

By the time we reach the end of the long, winding road, snowflakes have begun to hit the windshield, icing the glass. It makes it almost impossible to see. Uriah flicks the defrost switch on in the pickup cabin, but it only does so much. The temperature outside is too cold.

"We should stop," I say.

"We can't," Uriah replies, clutching the steering wheel. "Once that blizzard hits, these roads will be packed with snow – and there's nobody left to clear the highways. We've got to keep going."

I take a deep breath.

"Okay," I say.

As we drive, we roll onto a road that parallels a huge meadow. Large stumps litter the open space – now covered with a blanket of ghostly white snow. It is early morning, but it's dark. The sky is covered with thick, black clouds.

"Cassidy," Uriah says, his voice quiet – despite the fact that nobody is in the car aside from us. "Have you thought about what the Alliance is going to do without those recruits from Sky City? We were counting on a few thousand soldiers to back us up. Omega will come back, and we don't have enough men to combat their force of foot soldiers."

"We'll improvise," I tell him. "The patriots did it during the Revolutionary War, right? A bunch of guerilla fighters against the biggest army in the world at that time – Great Britain. If they did it, we can, too."

"Yeah, but they had powerful allies," Uriah counters. "France supplied us with all kinds of help."

"We'll have to make do with what we have," I say. "We've got Canada and Mexico on our side."

"Neither are exactly leaders of war, but yeah." Uriah eases onto the highway. The road is abandoned – much to my relief – and slick with ice. "We need somebody freaking savage. Somebody who is just as ruthless and desperate as Omega."

"We're pretty desperate," I say.

"But we're humane," Uriah points out. "We don't enslave people, and we haven't been planting terrorist cells around the country, preparing children from a young age to destroy the enemy. We're new to this game. We need someone who isn't new. Somebody who's got power and influence."

I think about this.

Uriah is right. We do need an ally that is stronger than the Pacific Northwest Alliance. We need somebody with weapons, training and a thirst for vengeance. Somebody who hates Omega with a passion. Somebody who would be willing to go the extra mile to take them down – more than just a coalition of states. More than the Pacific Northwest Alliance.

Something more terrifying.

Something that equals Omega in terms of intimidation.

Something that can't be found in California. Something beyond a place like Sky City. That kind of thinking is too small. We have to think big to win this war.

We have to think global.

"You're right," I say after a long silence. "But I don't know who that would be."

We drive through the early morning. The wind becomes stronger. Snowflakes fall in dizzying swirls, coating the cars and swarming across the road. Everything becomes crunchy and slick. We drive slowly to avoid sliding on the icy pavement.

"We're almost there," I say. "Gotta be."

I look at Uriah, and I realize something: coming back to Camp Freedom is like a homecoming for him. Uriah is a Mountain Ranger, a lieutenant who was under my father's command when the group originally banded together right after the EMP.

"Where are you from?" I ask. "I mean, before all of this. How did you get involved with the Mountain Rangers?"

In all the time that we've known each other – all the missions we've been on together – Uriah's past has always remained a mystery. My knowledge of him is based solely on his performance as the best sniper in the militia, a deadly and skilled soldier.

But who he was before the EMP?

I really have no idea.

"I lived up here," he answers.

"In the mountains?"

"Yeah. I had a house. It belonged to my...family." He pauses. "I inherited it. I was living there when the EMP went down and everything hit the fan."

"Where was it?" I ask.

"The middle of nowhere." He shakes his head. "It doesn't matter now. It's gone."

"What happened?"

The road curves and Uriah concentrates on navigating around a broken limb that has fallen into the path. When we've cleared the obstacle, we dive onto a tiny back road hidden in the trees.

Uriah apparently knows exactly where he's going.

Not surprising.

"It was burned," he says at last. "Omega burned it to the ground. I was hunting. Went out for a couple of days. I came back, there was nothing left but a plume of smoke and a pile of charred wood."

I hesitate before I ask, "What happened to your family?"

He clenches his jaw and turns up the heater in the cab.

"Your father and the Mountain Rangers saved my life," he says, avoiding answering the question. "Once upon a time, before all this, I was trained as a small-town cop in a one-horse town in the Central Valley." He shakes his head. "Life happened. I ended up moving into the hills. Stayed there." He frowns. "And then *Omega* happened, and here I am. Camp Freedom was the best thing in my life. Your *father* was the best thing."

"He was honest and fair," I agree. "He was a good leader, like Chris."

I bite my lip.

"I'm sorry he's not here," Uriah says. "The Rangers miss him."

"Me too," I agree.

I doubt the pain of that loss will ever leave me.

"We're almost there," Uriah announces, changing the subject. Avoiding the entire conversation of what happened to his family – if he even *had* any left before the EMP.

I may never know.

As we continue, a gray light spreads across the forest. The snow is really falling now, turning the muddy roads to slush. I pray we don't get stuck in a rut and have to pull any of our vehicles out.

But I recognize much of the scenery – despite the fact that most of it is covered with snow. The sky is white, the air is white, and the ground is white. I feel stuck in purgatory, a speck of darkness against a giant sheet of paper. It's unearthly, and I'm just glad I don't have to trudge through it on foot.

I've done *that* before. It seems like ages ago when I was last roaming these hills, searching for my father with Chris in the dead of winter, before I knew anything about Omega. Before I knew how to pick up a gun and fight.

I don't even know who that girl was.

Was she really me?

I look down at my hands. I've killed so many people since then.

The Cassidy Hart that was born in Los Angeles is gone.

Someone new has taken her place.

"Holy crap," Uriah mutters.

Up ahead, I see the gates of Camp Freedom. The chain link fence and barbed wire surrounding the perimeter are still intact. The wooden sign that heralds the camp's name is still standing, dusted with icy flakes.

There are guards posted inside the guardhouses, protected from the harsh weather. They run out into the snow as we roll up to the checkpoint. Uriah opens his door.

"Uriah True?" the guard says, shaking his head. "I don't believe it!"

"Sam," Uriah replies, grinning. "Good to see you."

I don't know Sam, but Uriah seems very happy to see him.

Somewhere down the line in the convoy, I hear Commander Jones' voice. It's impossible to make out what he's saying above the howling of the wind, but I don't need to. Once the guards verify his identity, they open the gates.

Uriah gets back into the truck, still smiling.

"Sam was a good friend of mine," he tells me, pulling through the entrance. "He was another one of the original Mountain Rangers."

The Headquarters building is still sitting in the same place to the right. There are very few people in sight, aside from the militia guards milling around as we park the convoy in front of the General Store.

I tighten my jacket and open the pickup door. The wind is freezing. Icy chips slap my cheeks as I walk around the back of the truck. Uriah is bundled up in a hood and jacket.

My team and the Rogue Rangers empty from the convoy, heading to the Headquarters building. I feel like I'm walking through a dream – reliving a memory. This is a place I am so familiar with, but it looks like an alien planet in the midst of this blizzard.

How odd to come full circle – back to the place I was forced to leave when I joined the National Guard. When I left my family and friends behind to fight Omega on the front lines.

And here I am again.

I climb the wooden steps to the Headquarters building, pushing the door open. There is no one inside. A single lantern casts orange light against the walls. There's an empty table in the center of the room – again, a familiar object. I remember walking into this place and meeting Angela Wright for the first time.

I remember bringing Colonel Rivera here when he came to the mountains, seeking recruits for the National Guard. I remember my father, arguing with Chris about what would happen to California if the militias won the war.

Three people I've known.

Three people who have died.

Manny walks in with Arlene, stomping his boots on the floor.

"I'd say it's a little chilly outside," he exclaims. "Anybody care to build a snowman?"

Elle follows him, dusting snowflakes off Bravo's shiny coat.

My small team and the Rogue Rangers gather inside the room, Commander Jones walking to the front of the table. He looks exhausted – old. Dark circles cling to the hollows of his cheeks. His eyes are bloodshot, his enormous shoulders hunched.

"We finally did it," he says, his voice raspy. "The insurgency camp has been eliminated, and everyone here performed with courage. We have suffered no casualties." He bows his head. "Thank you, soldiers. Go rest."

I am about to say something when the door to Headquarters opens. A man walks inside, his dark skin gleaming against the lamplight. He's in his sixties, tall and broad.

"Commander Buckley," I say, recognition dawning.

"Cassidy Hart?" He blinks. "What are *you* doing here?"

I offer my hand and he takes it, grasping it firmly.

"It's good to see you again, sir," I tell him. "It's been a long time."

He looks dazed, his eyes falling on Manny, Uriah and Vera.

"How is this possible?" He looks at Commander Jones. "Jones, what's going on? I haven't heard so much as a whisper from your team in weeks."

Jones places his hand on Manny's shoulder.

"We've been reunited," he says. "Commander Hart and her team were fleeing Sky City when we came across them in the high mountains. They helped us locate the insurgency camp – it is no longer a threat."

Commander Buckley raises his eyebrows.

"Sky City exists, then?" he asks.

"Unfortunately, yes," I confirm. "We've been betrayed. Omega has infiltrated the base – they control everything that goes on there. We barely escaped with our lives."

"Where is Commander Young?" Buckley pursues. "What happened to Angela?"

"My mother is dead," Vera says, her voice sharp.

"I'm truly sorry to hear that, Wright," Buckley replies. "Truly."

"Commander Young is in Monterey, defending the coastline from Omega's troops," I tell him.

"Hold up there," he says. "*Commander* Hart? Last time I saw you, you were a lieutenant."

"She's a senator now, too," Manny volunteers. "Better tip your hat, Buckley. Show some respect."

Buckley rolls his eyes.

"I see you haven't changed a bit," he replies.

"Thank God," Manny comments. "At least I haven't lost my sense of humor."

"Only your sense of sanity," Buckley quips, a good-natured smile on his face. "So it's true what they've been saying about you and Chris Young – and the Freedom Fighters. You were at the coast, yes?"

"The Battle of Monterey ended no less than a week ago," I say.

"Incredible. How is it looking over there?"

"Desperate," I admit honestly. "I was hoping to recruit troops in Sky City – but it was a trap. There's nothing there for us. Sky City is a dangerous place."

"A place that needs to be eliminated at some point," Uriah agrees.

"But not tonight," Jones interjects. "My men are exhausted and starving. They need to rest."

"I agree," Buckley says. "But before you leave, you said you reached your objective after all this time? You destroyed the insurgency camp?"

"Thanks to Arlene Costas," Jones acknowledges, nodding toward Arlene.

"Costas?" Buckley looks between Manny and Arlene. "You married this maniac?"

"I'm afraid I did," Arlene says, offering a weak smile.

He shakes his head.

"And this is my niece, Elle," Manny says.

"Wow. A whole family." Buckley shrugs. "I never knew you had folks, Manny."

"Amazing the things you learn during an apocalypse," Manny replies.

"You're one of the lucky ones." He looks at me, then. "And what about your father, Hart? Where is he?"

"MIA," I say tersely.

A pall falls over the room.

"I'm sorry to hear that, too," Buckley tells me. "Your father was a good man."

"One of the best," I agree.

More silence.

"The Youngs will be happy to see you, Cassidy," Buckley continues.

"So they're still here, then?" I ask, my heart lifting.

"They are." He pauses. "But...things have changed."

"How so?"

He shakes his head. "It may be better if you talk to them yourself."

I don't like the sound of that, but I say nothing.

"Since you've left," Buckley continues, "Camp Freedom has managed to survive against the insurgents.

About two months ago, they came out of the hills –
ambushed us in the middle of the night. Killed almost half
of us." His eyes darken. "It was a bad time. But we
survived. Since then, Jones and what's left of your father's
Rangers have been searching for them. I am amazed that
you were able to track them down and destroy them."

"They got what they deserved," I say, unflinching.

"There is a reason for your reputation, I suppose,"
he concludes.

"What reputation is that?" I ask.

He doesn't reply.

"I'd be more than happy to show you to the
Young's cabin," he offers.

"I know where it is," I reply. "But thank you."

I head toward the door. I am suddenly very tired.

My little team gathers around me, and it strikes
me then how lucky I am to have a group of friends like this.
These people are not just comrades – they are family.
Despite our differences or disagreements.

The war has forged in us a bond like no other.

"Sleep well, people," Desmond calls out.

I push the door open.

The snow is bitterly cold. I shield my eyes and trod
through the early morning blizzard. It's disorienting, so I
grab Uriah's arm as we trod through the slippery, icy road.

I look around. Everything is different – and it's not
just because of the weather. Several cabins are empty,
their roofs caved in, charred black. The remains of several

193

vehicles lie near a stretch of the fence behind the General Store.

The evidence of Omega's attack is still here. I shiver. Their touch makes the place feel tainted, somehow.

Strange.

We follow the road, walking in silence. Everyone is exhausted, too tired to speak. We come to the *Staff Circle,* a collection of cabins in a makeshift cul-de-sac. I spot the Young's cabin immediately, their familiar front porch, the same green shutters on the windows.

This is the closest thing to home I have left.

I hurry forward, climbing the steps. Uriah is right behind me, along with Manny, Arlene, Elle and Bravo. I hesitate, my heart fluttering in my chest.

Nervous? No way. I can't be.

It's just been too long since I've been here.

I knock. There's no answer. Several moments pass, and I knock again.

And then the door opens, and I smile.

"Surprise," I say.

Chapter Fourteen

Isabel's jaw drops. She is taller than when I saw her last, almost as tall as me. Her wild blond hair sticks out in every direction – as always – and she is wearing standard-issue refugee supplies: coarse blue jeans, boots and a thick sweater.

But it's her face that's changed.

Her left cheek and eye have been completely ravaged. Her left eye is milky and damaged, glassy and sightless. Her cheek is scarred, burned. A long, red gash runs from the bottom of her cheek down her neck, stopping at her collarbone. I am so shocked that I stand there and stare for a moment, totally at a loss for words.

"Cassidy!" Isabel exclaims. She flings her arms around my neck and pulls me close. "I can't *believe* you're here! I never thought I'd *see* you again!"

I embrace her.

"It's good to see you, sweetie," I say, kissing her forehead. "It's been a long time."

I step into the living room of the cabin, my team following on my heels. Isabel searches the small party, her face falling. She looks at me, her expression asking a thousand questions.

"Where's Chris?" she asks. "Where's Jeff?"

"Chris is safe," I say. "He's in Monterey."

"What about Jeff?"

I don't answer the question. I had not even thought about the fact that nobody here knows that Jeff is dead. For me, it has been a sad reality for so long that I have forgotten that not everybody knows what happened to him.

Instead I say, "We've got a lot to catch up on. We're all tired, Isabel. Where are Mr. and Mrs. Young?"

"Well, *I'm* right here." Mrs. Young stands in the doorway, a thick flannel shirt tucked into cargo pants. Her wispy gray hair is knotted in a bun. Her eyes are tired. But there is a huge smile on her face. "Cassidy Hart. My *dear* girl."

She hugs me tightly. It is a welcome embrace.

I feel safe here.

And then her smile falters as she looks around the room.

"Where are my sons?" she asks.

"Chris is fine. He's in Monterey," I tell her.

"And Jeff?"

I don't know how to tell her this. The burden of being the one to have to admit that her son is dead is a heavy one. It makes me sick inside.

"Jeff was killed in action," I say softly. "I'm sorry."

She stares at me. Her face pales.

"He died bravely," I assure her. "Fighting."

She lifts her fingers to her lips and closes her eyes, sinking into the couch in the middle of the room. No one says a word. Isabel sits beside her adoptive mother and rests her cheek against her shoulder.

Mrs. Young begins to cry.

I kneel down and take her hand.

"I did everything I could to save him," I say. "I swear I did. In the end, there was nothing anyone could do."

"I never wanted him to go to war," she whimpers. "With Christopher, it was different. He was born to fight. But Jeff…" She chokes on a sob. "He was just a child."

"He was a man," I reply. "And a good one."

The room echoes with her cries. It is torture for me, knowing that she will be eternally wounded – just as I am. The pain of loss will sting forever. It will fade, but it will always leave a scar.

"Where's your husband?" I ask. "I can tell him, if you want."

She looks up at me, peering through teary eyes.

"My husband," she whispers, "is dead."

"What?" I stand up, shocked. "How? When?"

Mrs. Young continues to cry. She no longer pays any attention to my words. Her sadness is too deep – too intense.

"It happened when the insurgents attacked," Isabel explains in a quiet voice. "They came in the night. I was asleep. They broke through fences and killed a lot of the people living in the cabins in the meadow." She bites her lip. "He went outside to try and help." She lifts her shoulders. "He never came back."

Manny sits down on the only other chair in the room.

"Damn them," he says. "Damn them all."

"I went looking for him," she goes on. "That's when this happened." She motions to her face. "I got caught in a fuel explosion. Stupid thing to do. I guess I'm lucky to be alive."

To steady myself, I turn to Uriah. "There are bedrooms upstairs," I say. "Everybody find a place to sleep. We'll sort everything out tomorrow after we rest."

He nods, leaning forward. He kisses my cheek.

I do not shove him away or reprimand him, because I know that there is no romantic intent in his kiss. It's meant to comfort me, and for that, I'm grateful. Vera walks to the creaky wooden staircase with Elle and Bravo. Manny and Arlene are right behind them.

They ghost out of the room, respectfully remaining silent.

I sit on the couch next to Isabel and slip my arm around her shoulders. I close my eyes.

And I sleep.

*

When I wake up, I am curled in the corner of the couch, a heavy afghan draped over my shoulders. The fireplace in the corner of the room is crackling. I sit up, feeling groggy. Isabel is cross-legged on the rug, staring at the flames.

"Isabel?" I say, orienting myself. "What time is it?"

It is dark outside.

"You've been sleeping since you got here," she replies. "It's almost two in the morning."

I rub my eyes.

"Wow." I look around. "Is everyone else sleeping, too?"

"Some of them." Isabel never takes her gaze off the fire. "Uriah went somewhere – I don't know where. Manny left, too. The others are upstairs, still."

"And Mrs. Young?"

"You can call her Margaret, you know." She sighs. "Calling her Mrs. Young makes her sad."

I slowly unfasten the buttons on my jacket, peeling away the filthy layer of clothing. My weapons and ammo are on the floor near my feet.

"Is she okay?" I say. "Is she sleeping, too?"

"Yeah." Isabel slowly gets off the floor and sits beside me on the couch. From my vantage point, her face is perfect – pale, with pinched, rosy cheeks and blue eyes. But when she turns her head, the injuries on her cheek and eye is visible.

It looks terribly painful.

"Can I ask you something, Cassie?" she says.

"Of course."

She hesitates. "Are we...are we winning the war?"

I inhale and rest my hands on my knees.

"That's a loaded question, kid," I answer. "The truth is, we're neither winning or losing. We're just fighting."

"So we're going to be okay, right?"

Her expression is desperate. She reminds me of myself.

I don't lie to her. She's felt the pain of loss – and the physical pain of injury. Omega has reached its nasty, poisonous claws into her life and ripped a chunk out of it.

So I don't tell her that it's going to be okay.

Instead I say, "We're going to fight."

She nods, understanding.

"Is there a place I can shower?" I ask. "I haven't rinsed off in a couple of weeks."

Isabel wrinkles her nose.

"Eww."

"My thoughts exactly."

She gets up. "I'll show you," she says.

I follow her through the lower level of the cabin. It smells like wood smoke and pine dust. It's a comforting scent. She stops at a large bathroom in the bottom level. "There's running water," she says, motioning to the shower. "And it's hot. Just don't use too much."

I muss her hair up.

"Thanks," I say.

She rummages around in a dusty cabinet in the wall, pulling out a bath towel. It smells like fabric softener. I take a long whiff and close my eyes.

"This smells like my house," I murmur. "I'm pretty sure I used to use this brand." I drop the towel on the sink. We light a couple of candles and Isabel tiptoes upstairs, bringing me back some clean clothes.

I start to close the door, but she stops me.

"It's good to have you back," she grins.

I lock the bathroom door and lean against it. There is a mirror, but I can't see much by candlelight. What little I *can* see is terrifying. I look like a feral animal, my hair matted, my face dirty and grimy.

I don't recognize myself. So I look away and undress, fiddling with the water faucet. The shower comes on and hot, steaming water spills from the spout. Heavenly. I jump in and let the water run over my hair, rinsing away the mud and gunpowder. Water dribbles into my mouth and rivulets race down my cheeks.

And then I grab the wall, dizzy, heart racing.

I shake myself.

This isn't waterboarding, idiot, I think to myself. *Man up. Or woman up. Whatever.*

But the uncomfortable, suffocating fear is still there when I get my head wet. I feel a rush of fear, and every memory of being tortured by Connor resurfaces, becoming real again.

At last, I stop fighting it and shut the shower off, standing there, naked and gasping for breath. Not my finest moment, but it occurs to me that maybe I'm suffering from some kind of trauma.

Before the EMP, it may have been called PTSD.

There's no name for it, anymore.

I step out of the shower and pull on a clean pair of black cargo pants and a white T-shirt. Against all odds, the gold chain that Chris gave me is still hanging around my neck. I kiss the shield and comb my hair out with my fingers.

It feels good to be warm and clean. It's such a luxury.

I put on clean socks, lace my boots, and step into the hall. It's probably only three o'clock in the morning, but that's okay. I slip into the kitchen and light a candle on the counter. I use the small flame to navigate through the cupboards. There is a lot of food here – canned goods and packages of sealed food.

I pull out a bag of potato chips and open them, and then grab a can of my favorite post-apocalyptic food – peaches. Chris and I shared many conversations together over a can of peaches. Back when we were foraging through houses in Squaw Valley to survive.

Before everyone I knew started dying.

You're so depressing, Cassidy, I think to myself. *Lighten up.*

But the thought remains true. I crunch on potato chips and savor the sweetness of the canned peaches in the silence of the kitchen. I enjoy the solitude. I am never alone anymore. There is always someone with me, watching me – or shooting at me.

Privacy is something that I sorely miss.

When I am done eating, I find a bottle of water in the cupboard and drink the whole thing. Words cannot explain how amazing it feels to be hydrated, fed and clean again.

There is literally no better feeling.

I go back into the living room. Isabel is asleep on the couch. I walk closer. She is grasping something in her hand. I kneel down and take a peek.

It's a bullet – and it looks like she took it from my ammo belt on the floor.

I rest my forearm on my knee. In sleep, Isabel looks like her childlike self. The girl that I used to know. But now she has changed – gone is the snarky little blonde.

In her place is a sad girl who has lost too much.

Not unlike myself.

I stand up and walk to the window. The curtains are drawn, but I peek outside. Icy frost covers the glass. As I close the curtains again, the front porch outside echoes with the sound of footsteps. The door opens and Uriah walks in. He is dressed in black, covered in white snowflakes. His eyes and cheeks are red, raw.

"Cassidy," he says, breathless. "Come on."

"Why?" I ask.

"You're going to want to see this."

He holds out his hand. I button my jacket and we walk outside together. He flicks a flashlight on, illuminating the darkness. It doesn't help that much – all it does is highlight the ice swarming through the air.

I hold tightly to Uriah's hand as we trudge through the snow, the slush soaking my pants. We are headed down a familiar path, toward the meadow. I remember this place in summer, when the plants were green and the temperature made me sweat.

When we reach the meadow, the familiar stretch of grass is covered in snow. Generator-powered spotlights are shining across the open space as militia soldiers frantically scrape away the last bits of snow. The blizzard is dumping more as fast as they can clear it, but there is a clear strip.

"It's Manny's airstrip!" I yell. "Why are they cleaning it up?"

The sirens go off. I close my eyes, remembering the first time I heard those sirens. At the time, I'd thought we were under attack. But they were only heralding the arrival of Manny Costas – who could be coming now?

The fear of the unknown keeps me rooted to the spot.

I hear the roll of thunder rumbling through the sky – I realize that it's not thunder at all. It gets louder and louder, shaking the ground. The lights from some sort of aircraft become visible.

I strain to see through the flurries of snow in the air. Although I am not standing on the meadow, the propellers from the plane send a wave of ice through the air. I shield my face with my arms.

The plane is huge, heavy. It's a C-7 Caribou. Its wide wings reach across the open strip of meadow, the propellers slicing through the air. The engine roars. My ears ring. The large, hulking metal mass roars down the meadow. It is impossible to hear anything above the scream of the engine and the turbo propellers.

It comes to a halt at the end of the meadow. The lights on the wings are bright. Militiamen from Camp Freedom hurry to help open the rear door. I walk to the end of the plane as the ramp in the rear folds down. There are soldiers inside the cargo area, and they are ready for war. All of them wear camouflage fatigues, bulletproof vests and ammo belts. They're carrying heavy guns.

"Who are these people?" I ask Uriah.

Commander Buckley appears from the blizzard and Manny is with him.

"These men, Commander Hart," Buckley says, "are a little something we like to call the Angels of Death. A special ops unit."

"That's dramatic," I reply.

Manny laughs erratically, a wide smile on his face.

"Welcome home, boys!" he yells above the howling wind and the sound of the propellers slowing down.

The men walk down the ramp. None of them look too thrilled with the miserable weather. But it's not until I see a familiar face that I understand Manny's excitement or Uriah's mysteriousness.

"ANDREW!" I cry, my heart lifting.

Andrew – my dear friend and one of the best snipers and techies on the planet. He is standing tall, radios on his belt and a backpack of supplies slung over his shoulders. He looks healthy – recovered.

I run forward and hug him.

"Commander," he says, embracing me. "It's so good to see you. Thank God you're here."

"I don't understand," I reply. "What are you doing here?"

"You said you needed help," he says. "We got your message on the radio."

I close my eyes, on the verge of tears.

"Thank God."

"You didn't think we'd miss it, did you? I'm the radio guy, remember?" He taps the radio on his belt. "But it's also miserably cold out here, so I'm going to cut this reunion short and head inside, if you don't mind."

"Of course." I hug him again. "I'm so glad you're okay, Andrew."

"Me too." He looks around. "Where's Vera?"

I smile. "She's at the Young cabin."

"Ah." He pauses. "Everyone made it out of Sky City alive?"

I sigh.

"It's a long story," I say. "I'll explain everything, I promise."

As the soldiers continue to come out of the plane, I recognize another man. Tall, dark and broad-shouldered. His hair is shaved down to the scalp, and a gold chain hangs around his neck.

"Alexander Ramos," I state. "What in the *world* brings you on this mission?"

He walks down the ramp.

"I heard there was a situation," he replies. "So I came."

"Last I saw you, you were in Sacramento."

"I hate the city. I was glad for an excuse to get the hell out."

His dark, serious demeanor is so typically *him*. It's refreshing to know that some people never change – it's comforting, in a weird way.

He exchanges a gruff handshake with Uriah and Manny.

"I see you're still alive," he remarks. "Good."

"Have you heard anything about my father?" I ask.

He says nothing. My heart sinks.

Alexander walks off. Uriah rolls his eyes.

"The sentimentality of that man is deeply touching," Manny says.

"You get used to it after a while," I joke.

I walk into the belly of the cargo bay. The seats are lined up parallel to the wall. About thirty men have emptied from the plane. I look around, my gaze landing at the end of the cargo door ramp. One man stands there.

Chris Young.

"Chris," I say.

I have never been more relieved to see him. I run down the ramp and collide with him, overwhelmed. Chris laughs heartily and gathers me to his chest, his strong arms closing me in. I don't even feel the cold anymore.

I don't even care.

He kisses me roughly and holds me at arm's length.

"I knew you'd be here," he says at last, his green eyes sparkling.

"How?"

"Because Camp Freedom is where I would have gone." He kisses me again. "I was worried about you, Cassidy. When Andrew got the message on the radio..." He closes his eyes and holds me tight. "It's a long story. Maybe we should go home first."

I trace my fingers down the sides of his cheek, his stubble coarse.

"I have a lot to tell you," I say. "So much has changed."

"I would imagine." He holds my head against his chest. "I love you, Cassidy."

I smile. Those words never get old. Ever.

"I love *you*," I say. "And I missed you. More than you know." I pause. "These past few days have been...difficult."

He nods. He understands.

He always understands.

Out of the corner of my eyes, I see Uriah standing, dark and still, swathed in wind and snow. He is watching us, a sad expression on his face. I lean my head against Chris's shoulder. I catch his eye and he looks away, taking several steps backward, and then disappearing into the storm.

*

We go back to the Young cabin. At this point, everyone is awake. Lanterns have been lit in the small living room, and Vera is clinging to Andrew's arm like a life preserver. Alexander sits on the edge of the couch, an annoyed expression on his face.

I have not forgotten that this is the man who loved Sophia Rodriguez.

Without her by his side, he seems incredibly uncomfortable.

Chris and I step into the room, brushing the ice off our jackets. Uriah is sitting on end of the couch opposite of Alexander, his gaze occasionally flicking up to Chris and me. He says nothing.

Elle tiptoes down the stairs, Bravo slinking behind her. She smiles broadly at the sight of Chris. "Commander Young," she exclaims. "You brought help!"

Chris places his hand on her shoulder.

"You bet I did," he grins. He scratches Bravo behind the ears. "Hey, boy. Looking good."

"Chris!"

Isabel sprints down the stairs and clobbers Chris, jumping on him like a toddler. Chris chuckles and spins her around in a circle. If he is shocked by the scarring on her face, he doesn't show it.

"Good to see you, Izzy," he says, kissing the top of her head.

"I can't believe you're back," she says. "I'm so happy!"

"Me too." Chris looks around the room. "Where's my parents?"

"Coming!"

Mrs. Young – or Margaret, as Isabel told me – comes down the stairs. She stops mid-step, staring at Chris. "Oh, my son," she says, covering her mouth. "Christopher!"

She descends the last few steps and Chris embraces her. As I watch, I realize just how fragile Margaret has become. Her skin is paler and she's lost weight.

"It's good to see you, mom," Chris says softly. He kisses her cheek. "Are you okay? How has life here been since I left?"

Margaret shakes her head.

"That's neither here nor there," she replies. "Cassidy told me about Jeff."

Chris's face falls.

"Ah." He takes a step back, his expression hardening. "That was some time ago. The Battle of the Grapevine."

Margaret squeezes her eyes shut. When she opens them again, they are glassy and full of tears. "Christopher," she says slowly. "Your father is no longer with us, either."

Chris shakes his head.

"No," he replies.

"I'm sorry, darling," Margaret goes on. "He died bravely…just like Jeff."

Chris takes another step backward, leaning against the wall. He presses his fingers against the temples of his forehead. An uneasy silence falls across the room. Margaret doesn't move.

"Life has been hard since you left," she says. "But we're still alive. And now that you're back, we have a chance to make Camp Freedom safe again."

Chris looks up. His eyes are red, but he does not cry.

He doesn't even shed a tear.

"I'm not here for Camp Freedom," he says. "I'm here to destroy Sky City."

*

211

Chris and I sit in the Chow Hall. I wanted to talk to him in private, and there was nowhere to escape to inside the Young cabin. The building is dark and quiet. It is now early morning again, and there is no one here. The big, open windows let plenty of natural light inside.

The buffet table is empty. The tables and chairs are abandoned.

Chris sits on a chair across from me, one leg propped up against a table. I fold my hands on the table and ask, "Have you heard anything about my father?"

"No." Chris sighs. "I'm sorry, Cassie. There's been no news."

I don't feel disappointed. I just feel numb.

"Andrew recovered quickly after you left for Sky City," Chris tells me. "He monitors the Underground radio waves. He got your message somehow, and he brought it to me. I knew what it meant."

"So you came for us."

"Yes." He clears his throat. "But I was being honest earlier. I came to destroy Sky City."

"Sky City is a metal box buried in the ground," I tell him. "It's almost impossible to penetrate."

"Impossible is a not a part of my vocabulary," he says, and grins.

"Chris."

He leans over and takes my hand.

"I brought thirty highly trained military operatives," he says. "We've got the manpower and the firepower. Believe me, this is not beyond our capabilities."

"Then I'm in," I say.

He nods, approving.

"There's something I need to tell you, though," he goes on. "After you left, we continued our interrogation of Harry Lydell. When we didn't hear from you for the first couple of days, I was already suspicious. I was ready to come get you then." He seems hesitant to continue. "As it turns out, Harry knows a lot about Sky City."

"He talked?" I ask.

"I made him talk." Chris leans back in his chair again.

"Ah, well, of course."

"He told me enough. So between his information on Sky City – the Omega infiltration and all that – and your radio message, there was no question. I was coming to get you, no matter what."

"But what about Monterey?" I ask. "Who's going to keep it safe from Omega? They could come back any day!"

"The Pacific Northwest Alliance is covering it until I get back," Chris says. "Anita Vega and her militia are doing a good job of protecting the coastline right now. Monterey will be okay."

I am not convinced.

"What are we going to do without more reinforcements?" I ask. "Sky City was a joke."

I tell him everything that happened – from the beginning. From Arlene's near-assassination to our imprisonment. I tell him how I was tortured by Connor and how Colonel Rivera sacrificed himself to allow us to escape Sky City. I tell him how we destroyed the insurgency camp with the help of the Rogue Rangers, and how I suspect that Sky City has been infiltrated for many years.

"Harry Lydell told us that Omega had infected every level of society," Chris says after I am done. "I'm inclined to believe him at this point."

"Me too."

Chris grabs the bottom of my chair and pulls it next to him, draping his arm around my shoulders. I lean against his chest.

"I'm sorry you had to go through that," he says. "Every time I let you out of my sight, something happens to you."

"I'm just a magnet for adventure," I quip.

"You're the source of every wrinkle on my forehead." Chris kisses the top of my head. "There's something else I need to tell you. You're not going to like it."

I give him a look.

"What?" I say.

"I brought Harry Lydell with us," he replies.

I bolt upright, on my feet, furious.

"What? *Why?*" I demand. "You can't be serious!"

"He knows things about Sky City that we don't." Chris shrugs. "He's a valuable source of information, and he can help us penetrate their defenses."

"Trusting a single word that comes out of that snake's mouth is suicide," I tell Chris. "You know that. Why would you take anything he says as truth?"

"Because Harry *is* a snake," Chris answers, standing up, facing me. "He'll do whatever it takes to stay alive. If you think he's loyal to Omega, think again. He's loyal to whoever will keep him alive, period. Trust me, interrogating him wasn't that hard. Harry fears death – he's terrified of it. He'll do anything to avoid it."

"I'll kill him," I say, cold. "Gladly."

Chris raises an eyebrow.

"Since when do you kill people gladly?" he asks.

"Since they ruin my life and kill my friends and family," I reply.

Chris grips my arms and holds me still.

"Listen to me," he says. "Don't you *dare* go cold. I know you've been through hell – we all have. But you especially. And I'm sorry. But don't lose that sense of humanity, Cassie. That's what makes you who you are."

When he says these words, his eyes glisten with unshed tears.

I have clearly hurt him, and for that I feel sorry.

"Chris," I say. "This is war. This is *death*. I won't pretend that I don't get satisfaction from making Omega pay."

"It's about preservation and defense." Chris lets go of me. "You know what? I'm sorry. I know what you're feeling. My father is dead, your father is dead. My brother is dead. Your friend is dead. Colonel Rivera, Angela Wright. Isabel…God, what happened to her? Poor kid. No child should have to live through something like that."

There is a moment of tense silence between us.

And then I say, "Omega doesn't deserve our mercy. You know that."

Chris remains silent. It's his way of saying, *You're right, but I'm still right, too.*

I press my lips against his, a slow, lingering kiss. When I open my eyes, Chris looks sad. He touches the side of my cheek with his finger.

"Don't ever change," he whispers.

"I won't," I say.

But it's a lie.

I already have.

Chapter Fifteen

Black. That's literally all I can see. All of us, dressed in black – black pants, jackets, vests and guns. My bright red hair is wrapped up in a black headband. We stand in the Headquarters building. A large piece of white paper is spread across the table in the center of the room. It's coming on late evening now, and there are more than thirty people packed into this small room.

I feel a sense of repetition.

We have done this before. We have planned missions and reviewed objectives. But the repetition is hollow, because some of the people I love the most are no longer with us.

Dad, Jeff, Sophia...

Vera stands next to me, her face expressionless. We both stare at the table, and Arlene, who is drawing details onto the map. She knows the layout of Sky City better than anyone...well, *almost* anyone.

"Let's bring in the devil, then," Manny says, leaning on the table.

Chris has his boot up on a chair, the crowded atmosphere of the Headquarters bothering him. I can tell from the look on his face – I know, because it is the same look that I have, now.

"Bring in Harry," Chris commands.

Andrew leans over the table and looks up at Arlene.

"So what we're looking at is a steel bunker buried deep into the heart of the mountain," he says, "with an airtight, sealed entrance, and dozens of patrols and snipers hidden in the woods. Sounds like a great party."

"I'll bring the drinks," Vera deadpans.

"Deal," Andrew grins. "And I'll bring the appetizers."

The door opens and several militiamen bring Harry Lydell into the room. He looks tired. His complexion is pale, his blue-gray eyes bloodshot. The left side of his face has been mottled with dark, purple bruises. His uniform is wrinkled.

"Ah, an audience," he purrs. "How theatric of you."

The guards have him stand at the end of the table, in full view of the room. I realize that, even as a prisoner, Harry feeds off the energy of others' attention. And I'm not sure if I pity him for that – or if it just makes him pathetic.

"Cassidy," he says slowly, his gaze lingering on me. "Don't you look dangerous tonight?"

In the back of the room, I see Elle slip in with Bravo – and Isabel is with her. Isabel whispers into Elle's ear and Elle smiles, and they stand near the edge of the crowd. Elle's laser-like gaze stays on the map and Harry.

She misses nothing.

"Let's get to the point," Uriah says, annoyed. He rests his fingers on the edge of the table. "Arlene?"

Arlene clears her throat and looks around the room.

"If you want to destroy Sky City," she says, "You'll have to go to the core. The bunker is designed like a hive, with ring upon ring of security, diving deeper into the ground. Cassidy – you and some of your men have been inside now, so you understand what I'm saying." She looks at Chris. "Once you get inside, there will be troops everywhere. The downside is that you will be invading a steel box of hostiles. The upside is that they can only come at you a little bit at a time. Most of the troops are located on the first level. The thirteenth level is where you want to go."

"Why the thirteenth?" Chris asks.

"The Communications Center is located there. And so is the arsenal." She smiles slightly, sharing a knowing glance with Manny. "Let me put it this way, Commander. If you can take out the Communications Center, you can take out their contact with every single Omega base from here to China. And you can hack their files."

I perk up.

"I like the sound of that," I say, and smile.

"I knew you would," Arlene replies. "But this is where we come to a speed bump." She stops to look at Harry. "The Communications Center can immediately call for backup anywhere in the world – this is where Omega has trumped us. Their access to and use of technology gives them an enormous advantage. But, they are not invincible. During my time at Sky City, even *I* knew that the base communicated with the outside world because of a radio tower that was hidden in the mountains." She clasps her hands behind her back. "Take out the tower, and they can't call for help. You will have a good ten minutes to get inside the base before they boot up their satellite comms. If you can get to them before they can do that, you'll be fine."

"And they won't be able to communicate with the patrols outside the fences," Vera adds. "Or the snipers."

"Exactly," Arlene confirms.

"So before we do anything else, we've got to take out the radio tower," I say.

"Yes."

"Where is the tower?"

"It's only a half a mile from the base," Arlene says. She draws a circle around a spot in the map. "It's here. On top of a rocky crevice. You'll be able to see it clearly."

"Okay, so we take out the radio tower," Uriah replies. "Then what?"

"We take out the snipers," Chris answers. "And the guards. It shouldn't be a problem for us."

"It won't be," I assure him, a half smile on my face. "We can take out all the patrols and snipers. But how are we going to open the airlock? Sky City's got two steel doors. One in the front and another right before the entrance to the bunker."

"Door breach," Andrew explains. "Don't worry. I'll take care of that. We'll bring breachers for each entrance."

220

"Good." Chris taps his finger on the map, looking at Harry. "Okay, Harry. Tell the room how you've visited Sky City. Tell them what you told me in Monterey."

I wonder what information he could possibly offer.

What could possibly be important enough to bring Harry here?

"When I joined Omega," he says quietly, dramatically, "One of the first places they brought me to was Sky City." He wipes his hands on his pants, as if cleaning them. "I was impressed by Omega's masterful infiltration of an organization that had once been so...*pure.*"

A chill slides down my spine.

"As I understand it, Omega began seeping into Unite and Sky City at least ten years before the invasion." He shrugs. "Their takeover wasn't complete until after that point. And now they control it all."

"Not for long," Andrew mutters.

"You really think that destroying *one* base will bring down the whole of Omega?" Harry snorts. "There are thousands of Omega strongholds across this country – across the *globe.* You're so grotesquely outnumbered, it's almost comedic."

His words resonate, casting a pall over the room.

"And you, of course, would know all about being loyal to Omega," Chris says at last. "Because you've been giving up their information to us to save your ass from a firing squad." He shakes his head. "You and everyone else in Omega – you're all the same. And that makes you weak. It's not about the group – it's not about the *team* to you people. It's about making yourself better. Making yourself wealthier. Making yourself more *powerful.*" He shrugs. "It will be your downfall."

"Omega will welcome me back with open arms," Harry says.

"What makes you think you're going back?" I demand. "What makes you think that I won't just pull out a gun right now and throw a shot right between your eyes?"

Harry looks stricken for a moment. Surprised.

He collects himself and replies, "Because, as you've said yourself so many times...you're not like us."

I glare at him.

Just watch me, I think. *I wouldn't even hesitate.*

"Which brings me to the reason Harry is here in the first place," Chris says, his voice booming in the small room. "He's going to open the front door to Sky City for us."

"Wait...what?" I say.

"Colonel Rivera – when he first brought you into the bunker," Arlene says, "He used a hand recognition scanner to open the airlock."

I remember.

"Harry's position as a District Prefect and General has granted him access into Sky City before," she continues. "And it still will. We don't have to breach the first door."

222

"Just the second one," I say.

"That's right."

I tilt my head, finally understanding why Harry is still here. Why he's still alive. And why Chris hasn't thrown him across the room by now.

Because he can actually make our job a little easier.

"How are we going in?" Vera asks.

Chris flashes a brilliant smile.

"The fun way," he says.

*

"I'm pretty sure you and I have very different definitions of fun," I say, horrified. I'm standing in the Chow Hall with the rest of the operatives. The tables and chairs have been cleared out, and Chris's team is lined up.

Chris is holding an oxygen mask in his hand, along with a black vest and backpack.

"Okay," he says simply. "Let's go over this one more time. This is the oxygen tube, and *this* is the rip cord that will deploy the parachute." He motions to a three-ring cord on the side of the vest. "Don't pull the oxygen cord. Most of you already know this, because many of you are SEALS, like me." He looks at me. "And yes, Commander Hart. Our definitions of fun *are* very different."

"I don't think I can do this," I mutter.

We have been going through "ground school" for the last three days. It seems like such an achingly long amount of time to prepare for a mission, but this is something that cannot be taken lightly. Although many of the operatives of the Angels of Death have jumped before – I have not. And neither has anyone on my team.

Uriah stands on my right, Vera on my left. Andrew is beside her, and Alexander is beside him. "HALO jumping is easy," Andrew replies in a quiet voice. "You just have to make sure your oxygen is working or you can lose consciousness and forget to pull the parachute cord."

"Fantastic," I say.

"And jumping from a high elevation will be a freezing experience," Vera adds. "We'll have to keep warm, or we'll be ice sculptures when we hit the ground."

"That should be familiar territory for you," I say.

She gives me a look.

"Sorry," I shrug.

But not really.

Chris reviews the basics of deploying our chutes one more time – a small drogue chute is deployed first, catching the air, and then ripping the main chute out of our packs.

I'm nervous.

Yes, I have been through worse. But jumping out of an airplane and parachuting into enemy territory is not something I have ever aspired to do.

Ever.

"What happens if the chute malfunctions?" I ask.

"Then you die," Alexander states.

"Gee, thanks."

"It's true."

"Whatever." I look at Chris. "Tell me there's a failsafe for a chute malfunction."

A couple of people in the back of the room chuckle.

"Yeah, I hear you back there," I say, annoyed. "When you're screaming without a chute for a twenty-thousand-foot fall, tell me how funny you think *that* is."

"The chute *is* the failsafe," Chris tells me. "You get one chance."

I nod.

"Okay, then," I say. "That's what I wanted to know."

"Just watch me," he goes on. "Do exactly as I do, and you'll be fine."

Great. I get one shot. If I blow it, I die.

Wonderful.

"For those who don't have experience with HALO jumps," Chris says, turning his attention to me, "you're about to learn on the job, and these three days of intensive training have prepared you well for it. HALO jumping - High Altitude Low Opening. Basically, you're jumping from a higher elevation. For us, that'll put us at about twenty thousand feet, although most HALO jumps are around thirty thousand."

We have gone over the jump dozens of times, each of us practicing pulling our ripcord, falling and landing.

The team scatters into groups and Chris straps the vest and pack to my back. "Where's the ripcord?" he asks.

I close my fingers around the cord on the right hand side of the backpack.

"Pull," Chris commands.

I do.

"Good." He gives me an approving smile. "These vests don't have an automatic chute deployment system – but it does have an altitude tracker." He taps a small device attached to the pack. "When you reach a certain elevation, this thing will start screaming at you through the helmet. That's the signal to deploy the chute." He shrugs. "Or you can just use your common sense."

I roll my eyes.

"You're so comforting," I say.

"That's what I'm here for, baby." He kisses my forehead. "Come on. If Vera can do it, so can you."

"Don't compare me to Vera," I warn.

Chris closes his mouth, offering a sheepish grin.

"Right…" He leans closer. "Look, Cassidy. This is dangerous. You're a damn good soldier, everyone here knows that. Manny's going to pilot the plane that takes us in, and you can stay up in the air with him and monitor the mission."

"You know I'm not going to do that," I say. "You fight, I fight."

He sighs.

"I knew that's what your answer would be," he tells me.

He knows me too well. As much as I would like to stay with Manny in the plane – I can't. My job is to make sure my team secures the objective. I have to be an active part of that.

I'm a fighter, and nothing can change that.

Not even fear.

Going on a crash course for parachute jumping is not my idea of a good time, but there is no other way to get into Sky City undetected. Our first priority is to take out the radio tower so that we can infiltrate the bunker. We can't reach Sky City by vehicle. We can't land on the airstrip that Manny once used.

Coming in by air is the only way.

"HALO jumps are fun," Chris says. "I used to do them all the time."

"Yeah, well," I reply, "you're kind of insane."

"Nah. An adrenaline junkie, maybe. But not insane."

It is now completely dark. Almost zero hour.

"What happens when we're done with this mission?" I ask.

"We go back to Monterey," Chris replies.

"Without recruits?"

"The Alliance will have to do for now."

I am not so sure.

The Alliance and the militias are struggling without backup. This war is getting tight. Without extra recruits, we may not survive the next wave of Omega troops.

"Almost time to go," Chris says.

Alexander walks across the room, looking at Chris.

"We're good to go," he tells him.

"Good." Chris holds out his hand. "It's good to have you back, Ramos."

Alexander shakes Chris's hand – there is a flicker of emotion on his face, and then it vanishes. I think Sophia's death has been harder on him than he would ever admit.

"How is Derek doing in Sacramento?" I ask Alexander. "Did you see him before you left?"

"He was healing up," Alexander replies. "I imagine he'll be battle ready in another couple of weeks."

Good to know. I had been wondering about Derek.

Commander Buckley walks through the door to the Chow Hall, his dark eyes glistening in the faded light.

"You've got a green light," he says, his baritone voice filling the room.

Commander Jones is right behind him. He looks at me, sadness in his eyes.

Chris takes a deep breath, looking around the room. Most of these operatives are strangers to me – soldiers that Chris brought with him out of Monterey.

"Let's go take out Sky City," he says.

I swallow a massive lump in my throat.

I don't know what's coming next. Whatever it is –
it's going to change everything.

I just know it.

Chapter Sixteen

The cargo bay of the C-7 Caribou rumbles and rattles like the inside of a tin can. I sit on webbed nylon, a stretchy net. My hands grip my vest. The lights are dim and dull. The operatives are lined up on each side of me and across from me. Chris is on my left, on the end. Elle is in the cockpit with Manny and Bravo – she will not be allowed to participate in the HALO jump. She is a little too young for this.

Arlene is staying behind in Camp Freedom, monitoring our progress via radio. Harry Lydell sits on the edge of the bench across from me, silent and pensive. He seems about as thrilled to be here as I am.

Which is not very.

We all have earplugs smashed into our ears, the rumble of the aircraft deafening. We have to shout directly into one another's ears to even be heard.

"It's loud in here!" Vera yells at me, seated directly across on the bench.

That's a gross understatement.

The four propellers on the massive wings echo throughout the cargo bay. The engine roars. A small radio is clipped to my vest, the earphone shoved deep into my ear. "Ready, Freddie?" Manny's voice crackles.

"Nope," I reply, dipping my chin to make sure my voice hits the speaker on my vest. "But go for it anyway."

"I plan on it! Bombs away!"

His hysterical laughing stops as he cuts off the transmission. I steal a sideways glance at Chris, calm and cool – as *always*. My heavy pack of weapons and gear is weighing my shoulders down. A tactical helmet is strapped tightly to my head, an oxygen mask and tube hanging to the side of my face, ready for the jump. On top of that, I've got the parachute attached about mid-chest level. For Chris, it's not a big deal. For a small girl like me, I feel like I'm giving a piggyback ride to an elephant. My heavy gear is packed into a kit bag right below the reserve chute. I'll drop it to earth about fifteen feet before impact. Because I'm small, my kit is small, too. The bigger gear bags stay with the bigger men on this mission.

Chris puts his hand on mine as Manny turns the plane around. We don't have that much of an airstrip, so his takeoff will have to be skilled and quick. I squeeze Chris's fingers. My stomach flips on itself. Not because of the flight.

But because of what I know I'll have to do.

The aircraft bounces down the meadow. I can't see anything – there are no windows here. I can only feel the pressure on my chest as the plane gains speed, bumping and accelerating, until we lift off the ground. I am pressed against my seat as we rise.

My ears plug up as we gain elevation. Because our starting point is Camp Freedom, our elevation has gone from roughly nine or ten thousand feet to fifteen thousand feet in just a couple of minutes.

It won't be long before we reach our jump point.

I take a deep breath, feeling sick. Honestly, nothing has ever scared me more than this. Slave labor? No big deal. Guerrilla warfare? Piece of cake. Countless firefights and a rescue mission into Los Angeles? A walk in the park.

But this? No. Just no.

"Breathe, Cassie!" Chris shouts, putting his hand on my knee. "You can do this."

I nod, too nervous to speak.

We continue our ascent until Manny hits cruising altitude, and the aircraft levels out. I inhale and exhale. We're at least twenty thousand feet up.

No big deal, I tell myself. *You're a tough girl. You can do this.*

I look at Vera. She is a pale shade of white and green.

At least I'm not the only one who's nervous.

"Listen up," Manny's voice crackles into my ear, "we're about five minutes away from the drop zone. When the prep lights flash, I'm going to open the cargo bay door. You check and double-check your gear. I don't want anybody taking a long drop with a short stop."

"You're not helping anyone," Vera yells, barely audible.

Chris and I double-check our gear.

"Remember, arms out, legs out," Chris says, bringing his mouth to my ear so that I can make out his words. "Keep your appendages spread apart, you'll fall slower. Too fast and you'll get ahead of everyone. Stay with me and do exactly what I do!"

I nod. We've gone over this before.

I lean forward and kiss his cheek.

"If I live through this," I holler, "promise me we'll go on a real date sometime."

"A *date*?" he replies.

"Yeah. You know, like dinner and a movie? Kissing on the front porch?" I force a shaky smile. "All that romantic crap."

Chris takes my hand.

"You got it, kid," he promises.

Alexander looks at Vera, Andrew looks at me, and I look at everyone else. Chris pats my knee and then straps his oxygen mask on. Everyone does the same, and suddenly I'm keeping company with a sea of faceless soldiers.

We are scary. We are dangerous.

Despite my terror, I am proud. The light in the cargo bay goes dark, and then everything is red. "I'm opening the cargo bay door," Manny says through the radio. "Stand back and enjoy the view, ladies and gentlemen."

The door slowly opens. I strap my goggles on, make sure my gloves are secured. It's too loud to hear anything, between the deafening noise of the engine and the screaming wind. From this point on I can only go through the motions of what we practiced.

The bottom door of the cargo bay levels out, forming a perfect jumping platform. I look out, into the night sky, and it takes my breath away. We are hovering just above the clouds. All I can see for miles and miles is a layer of white, and above that, the moon glows like an opalescent diamond, incredibly bright.

The Earth looks peaceful from up here. Like a glittering snow globe.

The light in the cargo bay turns green.

God, I pray. *I know I've begged you to let me survive before. But seriously. This time I really mean it. Please don't let me die. Not like this.*

I hope someone's listening.

Everyone in the room stands up. I do the same. We are perfectly lined up and spaced apart. I stand right behind Chris, staring at his parachute pack. I touch my own vest, feeling for the ripcord.

"Green light, go, go, go!" Manny says.

Chris and I are first. We are all lined up nose to tail, literally right next to one another. We will be falling in a stick, a diagonal line across the sky, staying close until it is time to deploy the chute.

I know that I cannot hesitate, because I could endanger the lives of the other jumpers. So I steel myself, say a prayer, and go for it. I let myself fall beside Chris into the open air. The sensation of falling is unlike anything I've ever felt, because it doesn't end after the first five or ten seconds. It keeps going, and I feel weightless.

I feel like I'm flying.

I keep my arms and legs spread out like a star, as I was told, and there is nothing but the night sky and me. There is no noise up here. The wind resistance cuts against my body, tossing me around like a kite. The oxygen in my air tank and mask keeps my lungs and brain pressurized. The temperature is numbingly cold – it must be far below zero. I am thankful now for the thick, bulky clothes and gloves.

The terrifying rush of adrenaline that I felt during the first few moments of the jump subsides. I am still scared, but now that the initial jump is out of the way – I feel better. All I have to do is pull the ripcord and float down to earth.

But these thoughts are lost to me as I tilt my head and look at the sky. The moonlight is reflected against the white clouds, making it seem like daylight. I see other jumpers spread out around me, dark, falling stars. We dot the night sky, silent, streaking toward earth.

If I weren't so focused on staying alive, I would say that it was beautiful, in a strange, unearthly way. I don't have time to dwell on it – it's only a passing thought. In just a few moments, we've reached the clouds. And then we're falling *through* them, and it is the weirdest thing I've ever seen.

And I say *weird* because I can barely describe it.

I feel like I'm floating through a fog cloud, cold air and water sticking to my skin and clothes. I am still falling, so the wind is still whistling around me, but I can't grasp anything. The cloud wisps right through my fingers.

We're out of the cloud.

The mountains are visible below. A mass of dark, connective groundwork covered in trees. I see a relatively clear, rocky space below. That is our landing spot, and, thankfully, I seem to be heading right toward it.

Let's keep it that way, please, I think.

Every time I blink, the surface of the Earth appears to be getting closer. The gut-wrenching rush of terror-made adrenaline that I felt when I jumped out of the plane is back. The momentary, paralyzing fear that my ripcord might not work – that my chute might malfunction – is very real.

The altitude tracker on my pack screams at me through the helmet. I reach my right arm behind me and my clumsy, cold, gloved fingers close around the ripcord. I pull it, and the drogue chute tears out of the pack, ripping the main chute with it. It catches the air above me and the straps tighten, catching my fall. The rings under my shoulders pull up and my legs snap downward. I am still moving down – and pretty quickly, too – but I'm not falling. I'm floating.

My pack of supplies drops below me like an anchor, drawing me down to earth again. I am hanging from the nylon straps. I grab the risers as I waft down to the earth. As I get close to the ground, I bend my legs and brace myself for contact. As soon as my boots hits the surface, I roll onto my shoulder, distributing the impact through my body, sparing myself the unneeded pain of broken ankles.

My parachute billows around me like a tent. I use the Capewell releases to escape the risers and quickly move to unbuckle my vest. My fingers are cold and clumsy. As I break free of the parachute, the rest of the team begins to land on the ground, too.

I step away from the parachute, dizzy, and unclasp my oxygen mask and tube. I take a deep breath and close my eyes. The terror is over – I am safe on the ground. My heart is still racing, but I feel great. I feel powerful.

I overcame one of my greatest fears.

I survived a HALO jump.

Thanks for letting me live, I think.

The parachutes billow on the dark, rocky plateau, like jellyfish washing up on the seashore. It's an odd sight, but every single parachute means that our men are making it through the jump. I take my helmet off and discard it.

Chris jogs up to me, his words quiet.

"How do you feel?" he asks.

"Like I just got off the worst rollercoaster in the world," I tell him. "Hyped."

"Adrenaline?"

"Supercharged."

"That's the energizer bunny I know and love." Chris kisses my forehead. "Let's finish this."

Vera fights her way out of her parachute, glaring.

The temperature is cold. Snow and ice cling to the rocks, but it is not snowing right now, and the weather seems pleasantly warm compared to the freezing temperatures of the HALO drop. The clouds are swirling around the rocks, hiding the presence of Sky City.

"That was fun," Vera states, a sour expression on her face. "Let's do it again sometime."

"Please don't make me laugh," I reply.

"Watch me."

As soon as every pair of boots is on the ground, we move out.

"*Sundog*, this is *Yankee*," I say into the radio. "Boots are on the ground. We're moving in, en route to Checkpoint Charlie."

"Copy that, *Yankee*," he replies. I can hear the smile in his voice. "How'd you enjoy the ride?"

"It's a once in a lifetime experience that I'd rather not repeat," I reply.

"What? Falling out of the sky and plunging toward earth with nothing but a parachute between you and death doesn't give you a thrill?" he replies.

"Not my idea of a party," I say.

"Boring, boring, boring." There is a brief pause. "Hang on, Arlene wants your ear."

"Team formation," Chris commands. "Follow my lead, we stick together, we keep it tight, and we keep our mouths shut. Let's go."

The silence of the forest is a stark contrast to the blistering speed and fear of our jump in. It's such a sudden change, I almost don't know how to handle it. It's not like I've been trained to jump out of planes – I'm just learning on the job.

We delve into the forest, threading our way through the trees. We keep our goggles on – they are night vision, and I can see what's going on around me. Everything is a clear picture of greens and yellows, illuminating the darkness. I am thankful for these handy tools, compliments of Commander Buckley and Camp Freedom.

The radio communication is connected to everyone on the team – when Arlene checks in, we can all hear her voice.

"All right, in about a half a mile, you will come to a clearing," she says. "Across the clearing, there will be a cluster of granite rocks, and in those rocks are more trees. One of those trees is *not* a tree – it's a radio tower. You've seen them before in cities. Large towers disguised as trees. From a distance it's hard to tell, but up close, they're as fake as a piece of plastic."

We keep moving.

"Once you take out that tower," she says, "you'll have about ten minutes to push your way to the entrance. They'll think it was a malfunction. They'll send scouts out to fix the tower. That's when you move in – you'll be close. The bunker entrance is just around the corner."

No one answers her. We have all seen the map. We know what it looks like. We know exactly where we're going and what we're doing – but it is always helpful to have someone walk you through enemy territory. Otherwise you can feel a bit lost.

When we reach the clearing, I spot the cluster of rocks across the meadow. There are trees there, too, caked with snow. "One of those is it," I whisper to Chris.

He nods. We move across the clearing as quickly as possible.

In the back of the pack, being watched by multiple militiamen, Harry plods along. He does not make a sound. He knows that we will kill him if he becomes a problem. If worst comes to worst, we can just use a breach blast to open the steel airlock of Sky City. Sure, it's the hard way. But it's better than having our location given away by Harry. It is this knowledge that keeps him silent.

When we reach the other side of the field, we gather at the base of the rocks, hiding in the shadows. Andrew sticks his head out of the group, breathing hard.

"I'll find it," he murmurs.

Vera rolls her eyes.

"He's such a martyr," she whispers. But there is pride in her voice. Vera is too fond of Andrew to mean half of what she says. Which is saying something, coming from her.

Andrew scurries up the rock, nimble and quick, looking over the rock formation. "It's up toward the top," he tells us. "I can disable it. Somebody cover me."

"I'll go," I say.

"Not without me, *hero*," Vera replies.

"Both of you get over there," Chris commands.

I climb up the rock, following Andrew over the curve of the granite formation. I don't like being up here, exposed. The moonlight seems too bright. I don't even need my night vision goggles. I push them up against my forehead, adjusting to the natural colors of the night.

We reach the base of a tree protruding from the top of the tallest rock. Up close, it's obviously fake. Nothing but a metal rod and strange, metallic branches. A small fence is built around the bottom. Andrew whips his backpack off and cuts through the fence with wire cutters, going to the base of the tree.

"So," Vera says. "The HALO jump. Thoughts?"

I raise an eyebrow.

"I've had better forms of evening entertainment," I reply.

Silence.

Then she says, "I was scared."

I look at her. "Who, you? I don't believe it."

She glares at me.

"I'm only human," she says. "And I'm not the ice queen you make me out to be."

I say nothing.

"I'm sorry, too," she tells me. "About your dad going MIA."

"Thank you."

"I know what it feels like."

She smiles weakly.

"Okay, if somebody could hand me the charges, that would be great," Andrew interrupts. We both look at him. He mutters under his breath and rummages through the backpack himself, taking the charges out – little more than a harmless binding of square blocks.

But only harmless in appearance.

He straps them to the base of the radio tower, checks his handiwork one last time, and stands up. "Okay," he says. "Let's go."

We scurry across the rocks, back to Chris and the rest of the team. Once we're safely clustered behind the granite, Andrew takes out the radio trigger. He holds it in his hand, looking around.

"Once this thing goes down," he says, "remember that we've only got about ten minutes to get to the front of Sky City. They'll be sending scouts to check out the radio tower. They won't be able to communicate."

He swallows and squeezes the trigger. The charges detonate. It's not a huge explosion – just enough to crack the base of the radio tower apart and fry the electrical wiring. The tall, metal tree crashes to the ground in a shower of sparks, a chute of light in the darkness.

"Go," Chris says.

We do. We spread out in teams, divided evenly between the thirty of us. Chris takes one team, Alexander takes another, and I take the last. Vera and Uriah are with me. Harry is with Chris's group.

We skirt around the cluster of rocks, delving into the thick net of trees. A bit of familiarity strikes me then. We are very close to the front entrance. I snap my night vision goggles back on and sling my rifle over my shoulder, keeping it locked and loaded, ready for use.

As we sweep forward, I can see the guard towers hidden in the trees. There are three of them situated like tree houses in the limbs. They remind me of duck blinds. In the darkness, they should be invisible, but I can clearly spot the irregular shape of the towers. I know, because I am a sniper, and snipers wait for me inside those towers.

Uriah and Vera are right behind my shoulder, and ten more operatives follow behind me. We are spread apart, covering all our flanks, but I hold up a fist and stop behind a tree. I sink down to one knee and peek around the corner, keeping my rifle secured against my shoulder, using the optics to find the guard tower closest to me. I take a deep breath, steadying myself, finding my natural point of aim.

The night vision makes the camouflaged guard tower look like a mass of green and black shapes. I pick out movement from somewhere up there – ever so slight. But it's enough. I squeeze the trigger and take the shot, using a special subsonic round for a stealthy kill - but the distinct sound of a body hitting wood tells me that I am right on target.

"Tango down," I say into the radio.

I take a couple of more shots, then move from tree to tree, peering at the next guard tower. Chris and his team have the first one covered, which leaves this one to my team.

Uriah kneels down. He's got this one.

He makes quick work of the guards inside and we move forward. As we near the tower, I take my night vision goggles off again. I am used to the darkness of the forest – it was my original training ground, after all. I feel more comfortable. This is where I belong.

With the natural light, I can clearly see the makeshift ladder rungs at the base of the trees beneath the platform guard towers. A gunshot zings by my head and I duck to the side. Uriah pops a few rounds into the bottom of the platform. There is a distinct *thump* as a body hits the floor.

"Sorry," Uriah says, and shrugs. "I thought I had them all."

It happens. At least the guard in the tower had terrible aim.

I quickly climb the rungs of the ladder and pull myself into the platform in the trees. Three dead Sky City troopers are on their stomachs on the floor, blood seeping from their chests. I kneel down and take the radio from one of their belts and listen. There's nothing but static.

Good.

"All clear," I say into my own radio.

"All clear," Chris returns.

We are good to keep moving.

I climb back down the ladder.

"Dead?" Uriah asks.

"As a doornail," I reply.

We don't waste time. Up ahead, I see the clear glint of the barbed wire fencing surrounding the entrance to Sky City. There are at least twenty guards. A large, white spotlight is illuminating the fence line. Lots of activity.

They know something is up.

We hover in the shadows, gauging the enemy's position. With no radio tower, they can't communicate with the guard towers. They don't know that we're so close. If they did, they wouldn't be lined up at the fence, waiting for us to take pot shots at them.

I lower my voice and talk into my radio.

"*Alpha*," I say, tagging Chris. "Let's clean this mess up."

"Roger that, *Yankee*," Chris replies, his voice muffled on the radio wave.

I turn to Uriah.

"Take them all out," I say.

My voice is cold and emotionless. Vera nods, checking her gun one more time. She ghosts a half-smile at me. This is something she and I both understand – something we both agree on.

I check my rifle one more time before we rush the fence, appearing from the forest like a tidal wave – catching the entire force completely by surprise. Taking down twenty startled guards with thirty highly trained operatives is an easy task, compared to the other things we've had to do.

I take out three guards, then two more. We reach the fence. I look up at the barbed wire coiled around the top. There's no way any of us are going to climb over that without being cut to ribbons.

"Back up, back up!" Andrew yells.

He sets a detonation cord at the base of a section of the fence and we pull back into the cover of the forest. When it detonates, it cuts a nice hole in the fence for us to enter through.

I sprint forward, the rest of my team hot on my heels, moving through the smoke, the taste of burnt metal on my tongue. By now, all of Sky City must know that we're coming.

The steel airlock built into the side of the mountain is as big and ominous as ever. The scanner to the left of the door sits there, glowing a dull red. Chris rests his rifle against his shoulder and gestures to the operatives in the back of the group. They drag Harry forward.

Always the dramatic one, he lifts his chin and slowly sets his hand onto the scanner. The pad glows green and there is a low hiss as the airlock opens.

"Access granted," Andrew says. "Nice."

Gunshots tear out of the entrance as the door swings open. I duck and roll to the side of the door. Omega guards in Sky City uniforms open a barrage of gunfire on us. The sound is deafening. I fire as many rounds as I can, peeking around the corner. Chris looks at me from the other side of the door, nodding.

"ANDREW!" I yell. "DO YOUR THING!"

He doesn't hesitate. He takes his backpack off, and I turn back to the entrance. Several brave troopers have pushed to the front of the passageway. I take a shot at the first one, hitting him right above his vest, near the collarbone. He twists and hits the ground. Uriah shoots the remaining two, and their enterprising adventure is over.

Andrew kneels close to me.

"Cover me!" he says, sweat rolling down his forehead.

I nod at Chris. Both of us jump into the open with our team, ripping through the Omega defenses with a wall of gunfire. Andrew runs forward and throws the backpack as far as he can. It slides down the passageway, and we immediately pull back to cover again.

Bam. The detonation makes my ears ring. I squeeze my eyes shut and wince. The pressure from the blast makes my brain feel like it's being squeezed. I force myself to breathe evenly, open my eyes, and struggle to my feet. I look around the corner. The passageway leading into the bunker is lined with dead Omega troopers.

More grenade launchers. Gunshots.

Bam, bam, bam.

I force myself forward, leading the way with Chris into the bunker. The dim orange lights illuminate the passage. The guard posts are abandoned. The guards lay dead on the floor. It smells of gunpowder and burnt human flesh. The second steel wall and door is locked shut. There is no scanner, no entryway.

"Give me an update," Arlene says over the radio.

"We're at the second door," I say, catching my breath. "There's no scanner. Not even a keyhole."

"Sky City was designed to be opened only from the inside once the second door was shut," she replies. "You'll have to breach it."

Everyone looks at Andrew.

"Apparently I'm the go-to guy for things that go boom," he remarks, annoyed. "I have no more flash-bangs.

But that wouldn't cut it anyway." He converses with some of the operatives in the group and comes out with two backpacks. "Time to light the birthday candles," he announces, a happy smile on his face.

"So you just carry bombs with you wherever you go, then?" Vera asks.

He sets the backpacks strategically along the steel wall.

"Basically," he replies, standing up. "I mean, it's what I do."

"Hate to break up the love fest," I say, deadpan, "but once we blast these doors open, all hell is going to break loose. There are a *lot* of Sky City troops in there. This blast will stun them and get them away from the entrance. But we'll have to move fast."

"Let's go for it," Vera says. "I'm ready, aren't you?"

"You'd better believe it," I reply.

High on adrenaline and anger, we back out of the tunnel. We wait outside until Andrew detonates the breach blasts, placed at strategic points in the metal. It will not rip it apart – but it can cut it. It's an incredibly strong explosion, unlike the first two blasts we've been present for tonight. It's earth-shattering.

I crouch on the ground with my hands over my ears and my eyes shut, trying to save myself from permanent hearing damage, or from getting shrapnel in my eyes. It takes a few moments for the smoke to settle.

"Here we go," Chris says. "Move in. On my command, I'll take the first shot. Shoot to kill. We are not on a mercy mission. We are here to wipe these suckers off the face of the Earth."

Chris's team moves in first, and I'm right behind him. I flick the flashlight attached to my rifle on, beaming it down the dark passageway. The orange lights are destroyed, and there is nothing but dust, dirt and smoke wafting through the air.

Chris's silhouette disappears into the tunnel.

Strangely enough, I'm not afraid. I'm calm.

Eerily calm.

By the time we hit the steel door, I am expecting another barrage of gunfire. But it never comes. The door is twisted and melted, flames lick around the ground, smoldering.

As we enter the bunker itself, I feel the familiar rush of cold, recycled air. The bright, white lights are flickering. Dead Sky City troopers are everywhere. Blood is smeared across the walls.

"These soldiers didn't die because of this blast," Chris says, looking at me, stricken. "They've been shot."

The ground is thick with dead bodies. It smells like blood. I keep my rifle tight, coming to the curve in the first level. The elevator in the center of the rotunda is jammed open, blocked by a dead man.

"What happened here?" Vera breathes.

"My guess," Alexander replies, "is that after you guys escaped, they started executing the Sky City troopers who were genuinely working for Unite. Made this place totally Omega."

I shudder.

How horrifying, to die in a metal box, trapped under the ground – murdered by the people who you thought were your friends.

"Arlene, is there a way to get to the thirteenth level without taking the elevator?" I ask.

"Yes," her voice crackles. "There's a staircase. Behind the barracks. Follow the rotunda and you'll see it."

We do. We walk, picking our way through dead bodies, the eerie silence of the bunker suffocating us like a blanket. Chris opens a heavy metal door. A huge staircase winds downward.

"Team formation," Chris says. "Keep your eyes and ears open. Just because everybody up here is dead doesn't mean everybody down *there* is."

He nods at me.

I press my lips together, and we slip down the staircase, fingers hovering over the triggers of our guns. We descend past the twelfth level, finally coming to a stop on level thirteen. Chris throws open the door.

It's abandoned.

Empty. There are no bodies. No signs of life. The steady thrum of the artificial air ventilation units feed the melancholy atmosphere. I feel chilled to the bone. This isn't right. Something is very wrong with this picture.

I can feel it.

"I don't like this," Chris says, echoing my thoughts.

"That's the cellblock," I reply, pointing to the left. "The Communications Center is to the left."

Harry – who has remained silent this whole time – laughs.

"Go ahead, open it up," he says. "You'll love what you find."

"He's served his purpose, right?" Andrew asks. "Can we kill him yet?"

Chris raises an eyebrow.

"Not yet," he tells him. "Soon, but not yet."

Harry frowns.

We walk through the rotunda, our footsteps echoing against the walls. The Communications Center is identified by a single metal door with two simple letters engraved on them: CC.

We don't have any trouble getting it open. Compared to the rest of the entrances that we've blown to pieces, this is a piece of cake. Chris is the first to enter the room. I'm next, followed by Vera, Uriah and Alexander. At least a dozen operatives stay in the hallway, covering us from behind.

The Communications Center is huge. Two platform levels look across at a wide room filled with desks and glistening computer screens. The screens are glowing. I stare, mesmerized. It's been so long since I've seen a computer.

In the back of the room, about a dozen Sky City soldiers are standing in a neat row, facing us. They have their weapons raised, ready to fire. I immediately hit the floor and duck behind a desk. Shots rip through the wood, riddling the wall with holes. I bring my rifle up to my shoulder and take out two of them. There's a wall of fire coming from them, though, and despite my best efforts, a couple of the troopers make it closer.

Chris sends a spray of bullets down low, razing across their legs. They fall to the ground, screaming, and the rest of our team picks up the slack. The troopers fall, one by one, dead. When the slaughter is over, I pull myself together and stand up, staring at the mass of dead bodies.

"They were waiting for us," Vera says, pale. "That was a suicide attack. They weren't even trying to survive."

"Maybe they were the last of the Omega troops," Uriah suggests, kneeling down, examining a dead woman on the ground. "They knew we were going to kill them either way."

I look at Harry. He stands in the back of the room, a horrified expression on his face. Apparently, he is just as surprised as we are.

"What do you know about this, Harry?" I demand.

"Nothing," he replies. "This is madness."

There is fear in his voice, and for the first time since his betrayal of the Freedom Fighters so long ago – I believe him.

Bam.

Alexander looks at Chris, then at me. He seems confused, dropping to his knees, a trickle of blood trailing from the side of his mouth. It happens in seconds, but the shock draws everything out – playing before my eyes in slow motion.

To the side of the room, in the corner, more shots are fired. Three of our operatives hit the ground, dead. I can't see the attacker. I shoot back blindly. The shots stop, but I don't see a dead body. I see Alexander keel forward onto the floor, gasping for breath.

And then, all I see is red.

I rise from the floor and sprint forward, toward the corner of the room. I see a flicker of dark movement, disappearing around the corner. I follow. The room here has a long, narrow hallway, lined with office doors. The lights are dim. The man fleeing from me is wearing basic combat fatigues, but aside from that, I don't recognize him.

He barges into the last door on the left. I follow. It's a huge office with another door behind the sterile desk and computer. He pushes through the door. I pursue, using my rage to fuel my muscles. The next room looks like the entrance to an emergency elevator.

Funny. Arlene never mentioned it.

Maybe she never knew.

The man realizes that he is cornered. I shoot him in the shoulder and he hits the wall. We roll onto the ground, a tangle of arms and legs. I jam my elbow into his cheek. I feel something crack. He screams. I bring my rifle around and hold the barrel against his throat, pinning him to the floor.

Connor.

I stare at him. Blood gushes out of his nose and mouth, dripping onto my hands, hot and sticky. His blue eyes dilate. He recognizes me. And all I see when I look at him is his cruel, twisted sneer as he held me under the water, torturing me for hours in the interrogation chamber.

Something snaps inside me.

I see everything that has happened to me since the EMP. In the blink of an eye, it all unfolds in my mind - every hurt, every horror, every loss. I reach around to the back of my belt, pull out my handgun, and hold the steel muzzle against Connor's forehead.

He spits up blood.

"You're going to kill me?" he asks.

"You just shot my friend," I reply.

"I am a soldier. Killing is my business."

"Guess what?" I answer. I squeeze the trigger. The shot rings through the small chamber, and Connor's body goes still. A bullet hole sits in the center of his skull. Blood drips from the side of the wound. His eyes stare at the ceiling, glassy and unseeing.

"It's my business too," I say, standing up.

I holster the handgun and sling the rifle over my back. Connor's blood slicks my hands and droplets run down my cheek. I don't feel satisfied. I don't feel proud.

I just am.

When I turn around, Chris is standing in the doorway. His lips are pressed into a thin line, his own handgun secured in the palm of his hand. I lock eyes with him.

He says nothing. I say nothing.

Tears burn like acid in the back of my throat. I bite my lip and walk forward. Chris steps aside. He does not offer comfort to me. Not a touch, not a kiss. Not even a smile.

I see something in his eyes that I have never seen before:

Fear.

We return to the Communications Center room in silence. Alexander is lying on his back, his eyes closed. His huge, muscled body is still, He is still breathing, but he is not conscious. Despite my best efforts, a tear slides down my cheek. I kneel next to him.

Don't die. Don't give up.

Every computer screen in the office suddenly glows white.

I look up, alarmed. Chris grips his gun. Uriah tenses.

The screens are synchronized in perfect unison. The blinding white of the screens fades, pulling back to a huge, white O. The screen becomes a picture – at first it is pixilated, and then it clears up.

It is a woman. A beautiful woman with milky white skin, long, black hair, and a dark red shirt. She is striking – intimidating. She sits in front of a white wall.

"Greetings," she says. "I trust that by now you have discovered that Sky City is no longer a threat to you. You have done an excellent job of destroying it, Commander Hart. I commend you for that."

I slowly stand, staring at the screens.

"Who are you?" I whisper.

"I'm so glad you asked," she replies, a calculated smile on her lips. "But first, let's talk about you. Shortly after you and your team cleverly escaped, Commander, the base was in an uproar. Those who were loyal to Unite clashed with those who were loyal to Omega. I'm afraid you exposed our corruption." She smiles again – and this time, it is predatory. Dangerous. "And so, everyone here is dead. I'm assuming you took care of the rest of the remaining soldiers?"

I say nothing. I look at Chris.

He doesn't return the gaze. He is staring at the screen, too.

"I'll take that as a yes," she purrs. "Ah, do I see General Lydell among you?" She pauses. "Very clever of you, using his handprint." She leans forward. "Unfortunately, you're all going to die, anyway."

"Who *are* you?" Chris demands.

My heart races. My mind spins.

This must be a trap. Someone is stalling us.

"My name is Veronica," she says simply. "Veronica Klaus. I am the International Chancellor for the organization that you have come to know as Omega."

My eyes widen.

A leader? An actual, living, breathing, leader?

"We go by many names, of course," Veronica continues. "But Omega is my favorite. Which is why we've been utilizing it so often lately. It's terribly catchy, don't you think?"

"How did you know we were here?" I ask. "Where are you?"

"You're so innocent," she laughs. "Like children." She tilts her head. "But maybe not all of you. You, Commander Hart, are a killer. I could use a woman like you in my ranks."

"I'd rather die," I hiss.

"Don't worry, darling," she replies, "You will."

I look around the room, searching for a trap.

"Don't worry, the base is empty," Veronica says, raising an eyebrow. "You've killed every last one of my men." She narrows her eyes. "You'll pay for that."

There is a long, heavy silence.

The satellite connection flickers, pixelating her image once more before clearing again. "You will never survive what's coming next," she warns.

"Where are you?" I ask again. "In the United States? Out of the country?"

"Does it matter? Darling, I'm coming to *you*. This war is almost over."

I wipe the blood off my hands, onto my pants.

"How do you know who I am?"

"I know about all of you," she replies. "Commander Chris Young. I must say, it's nice to talk with you again."

I stare at Chris, dumbstruck.

"*Again?*" I hiss.

He remains stoic, unflinching.

"And Vera Wright – your mother was Angela," Veronica goes on. "She's dead, isn't she?" She grins. "And Cassidy – how sad about your father. Missing in action, right?"

"Shut up," I warn.

"Or what?" she asks. "You'll reach through the screen and choke me? Please. Act like the soldier you are, Commander. Never make an empty threat."

Fear creeps into my heart. How does this woman know so much about us?

Where is she calling from? How did she know we were standing in this room?

Satellites, I think, chilled. *Arlene said it would take ten minutes for them to connect to the satellites after the radio tower went down...*

"I offer you a choice," she goes on. "All of you. The New Order will be established, and there is nothing you can do about it. So, you can fight valiantly and die – which I respect, by the way – or you can ally with me. Us. All of this fighting and death and gritty, dirty warfare. Day-to-day survival. It can end."

"Never," Chris says, and his voice is commanding.

"Think about it," Veronica says, sighing, ignoring him. "Give me an answer. I'll be in touch." She looks up, then checks a watch on her left wrist. "Well, now. It's time for me to say goodbye. Next time we meet, you will either join us, or I'll kill you all."

"But—" I begin, but she cuts me off.

"The end of this war has begun," she says. "Look outside. Everything has changed."

The screen goes black.

We stand there, looking at the black screen, shocked.

Nothing about this makes sense.

I look at Chris. He betrays nothing.

How does he know this woman? Or is she playing games with my mind?

Look outside. Everything has changed.

A dark, cold fist closes around my chest. I feel sick, as if something horrible has happened. I turn and run into the hall, past the elevator, into the stairwell. Chris is right behind me. We climb the stairs, reaching the first level. The first rays of daylight are breaking through the entrance to Sky City. We share a sideways glance.

Slowly, we begin walking up the passage. Air that is oddly warm touches my cheeks as we near the exit – a stark contrast from the freezing temperatures that were here. I step outside. The sky is gray, the clouds are thick. The sun is obscured, filtered through a dark screen.

I hold my hand out. The black, crusted flakes of dead souls stick to my fingers. It smells of smoke and death and horror. Chris looks stricken. Soon my hand is covered in black ash, and I wipe it off on my pants. It does little good, as it is coating my hair and skin.

I step back into the cover of the bunker passage overhang.

In the distance, the cloud cover is as black as night. It is a gray, colorless landscape. The swirling clouds around Sky City have been pushed away in a blast of sudden hot air. It stings my face and burns my skin.

Chris joins me and we look over the desolation together.

I swear I can hear the screams of millions of the dead.

Everything *has* changed.

Omega has gone nuclear.

Epilogue

When the end came, I survived. I was naïve. I did stupid things.

And then I learned to fight. I became a soldier, and I put the stupid behind me. I became smart. I moved quick. I played to my strengths and learned to crush my weaknesses. Because in war, weakness can get you killed.

I don't know what I am anymore. I am not weak. I am not superhuman, either. I am just a girl, fighting for survival in a world that has gone insane. So many people have died. I miss my family. I miss my friends. I miss the life I used to live – one of relative peace and relaxation.

I don't fear death anymore. I used to be afraid to close my eyes and never wake up again. Now, I would almost welcome the rest. I would never have to look over my shoulder again, wondering who was going to shoot me, or stab me in the back.

Now I face the world one day at a time.

I fight not so that *I* can live, but so that my friends can live.

I fight, because I am the last of those who are willing to stand up and hit back.

I fight, because that is who I am.

I am Cassidy Hart. I am vengeance.

To Be Continued in

State of Destruction

Book 7 of the Collapse Series

More Titles from Summer Lane:

Civilization, gone. Society, collapsed.

The apocalypse rules all, and mankind struggles for survival.

But there was a dog, and his name was Bravo.

Available on Amazon and Barnes & Noble.

A quest for survival. A friendship with a dog.

A girl with a sword.

The Zero Trilogy

Elle is just your average teenager...until the apocalypse destroys her world. Join her fight for survival in a world gone wild, featuring Bravo the bomb dog.

One girl. One dog. One sword.

Available today on Amazon and Barnes & Noble for just 99 cents!

Explore the universe of Summer Lane's Collapse with this eye-catching Illustrated Guide!

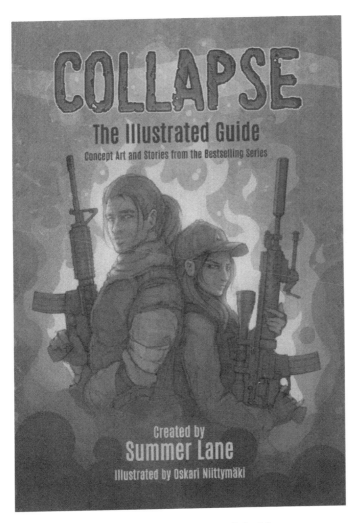

Collapse: The Illustrated Guide

Explore the world of Collapse for just 99 cents on Kindle and Nook – also available in paperback. More than 20 exclusive illustrations of beloved characters like Chris Young and Cassidy Hart!

About the Author

Summer Lane is the #1 bestselling author of the *Collapse Series, Zero Trilogy, Bravo Saga, Collapse: The Illustrated Guide* and the adventure thriller, *Unbreakable SEAL.*

Summer owns WB Publishing. She is an accomplished journalist and creative writing teacher. She also owns an online magazine, Writing Belle, where she has interviewed and worked with countless authors from around the globe.

Summer lives in the Central Valley of California with her husband, where she enjoys reading, collecting tea, visiting the beach and the mountains, and counting down the days until she has her very own puppy (if you've read *Bravo: Apocalypse Mission,* you'll understand).

Connect with Summer online at:

Summerlaneauthor.com

WritingBelle.com

Twitter: @SummerEllenLane

Facebook: @SummerLaneAuthor

Email Summer with thoughts or comments at:

summerlane101@gmail.com

Acknowledgements

As Cassidy Hart begins the last stages of her adventures, I have many reasons to be grateful. This is the sixth book of a ten part series – a series that has done phenomenally well so far and secures thousands of new readers every month. It has spawned The Zero Trilogy and other upcoming and yet untitled novels. That's the beauty of the world of Cassidy Hart – the story never really ends.

State of Vengeance was somewhat of a challenge for me to write, being that 2015 is the year that I have had to write five books in 365 days. The pressure was a little much, but I like to think that I'm a bit like Cassidy, in that every challenge makes me a better person, and a stronger writer.

There were many people who were involved with the production and editing stages of this novel. There is J.T. of Indie Editor, who sought out typos and grammatical errors with an eagle eye.

I would also like to say thanks to Steven J. Catizone, who designed a truly excellent cover for this installment. Thanks as well to Giselle Cormier, who always organizes releases and blitzes for me with the speed and efficiency that I need. Thank you to Don Lane, for pointing out tactical details, and for those radio call signs that Cassidy uses.

In addition, I am full of gratitude for the promotional artwork created by Oskari Niittymaki, always professional and always prompt. You will have the incredible pleasure of enjoying our collaborative work in *Collapse: The Illustrated Guide* when it releases in August of 2015. He's been great to work with. Thanks to Jennifer Lacey (Jen Eileen Photography), my lovely cousin who has done publicity photos for me since the beginning. Her talent for photography and warm light is unrivaled.

Thank you to my friends and my family (Mom, Grandpa and Grandma) for your support. There are too many to name, but I love you all. Special thanks to these generous souls: Ellen Mansoor Collier, my fellow writer and dear friend. David Hudiburgh, always a great proofer with a good eye for detail. Jessica, Lauryn, Rocklin, Denise, Miranda and Scott – you all add so much laughter and kindness to my life!

The mad rush of the first six months of 2015 is now over, and I am glad to be able to slow down just a little. With four more books scheduled to release within the next 14 months, I am looking forward to exploring the rest of Cassidy's story, and to expanding my horizons with the illustrated guide and more!

Last but not least, thanks to God. I felt that Cassidy's journey in this book examines the very nature of the potential evil of man – killing and vengeance. I am so glad that my God loves me, and that I am on His side.

Romans 12:19

Never take your own revenge, beloved, but leave room for the wrath of God, for it is written, "Vengeance is mine, I will repay," says the Lord.

Made in the USA
Middletown, DE
26 September 2018